Menace in the Night

Carolyn crept forward for a better viewing spot. Suddenly, someone laid a heavy hand on her shoulder. She was so stunned that she remained motionless for the vital minute during which she might have made her escape.

By the time she finally came to life and started to scream, the hand had yanked her around and clapped a sickly-smelling pad over her nose and mouth. She gave a stifled gurgle and fought for breath. Time telescoped in her mind; the sheer struggle for survival was punctuated by a panoply of Roman candles exploding behind her eyelids. Then the fireworks fizzled abruptly like a damp punk, darkness descended—and her body sagged to the ground. . . .

Kiss A Stranger

Glenna Finley

A SIGNET BOOK from
NEW AMERICAN LIBRARY
TIMES MIRROR

For My Mother

SIGNET, SIGNET CLASSICS, MENTOR, PLUME AND MERIDIAN BOOKS
are published by The New American Library, Inc.,
1301 Avenue of the Americas, New York, New York 10019

FIRST PRINTING, SEPTEMBER, 1972

5 6 7 8 9 10 11 12 13

PRINTED IN THE UNITED STATES OF AMERICA

Love conquers all.

—Quotation from Virgil found
in Cardiff Castle, Wales.

Kiss A Stranger

Chapter One

The gusty wind which was slathering rain over England's beautiful Somerset countryside decided to concentrate its efforts on a stretch of road near the regency city of Bath.

Directly under the deluge was a pint-sized British car containing a pretty American whose disposition, at that moment, was almost as steamy as the atmosphere outside.

"If you're pretending to be a car," Carolyn Drummond was addressing the dashboard irritably, "then you should have an engine that runs. Not one that starts coughing halfway up a hill and conks out at the top of it." She pounded with her fist on the steering wheel for emphasis and glanced around in desperation at the soggy landscape.

The group of black and white cows had gone

back to their breakfast grass after looking up in some alarm when she had coasted to a stop beside their pasture a few minutes earlier. A prickly hedgerow which fenced the meadow was as effective in keeping Carolyn out as it was in keeping the cows in. Not that there was any sign of an owner's house within sight anyhow.

Carolyn rolled down her car window and tried the direct approach on a mild-looking heifer. "You wouldn't happen to know where there's a telephone?"

The cow raised her head just long enough to bestow a disapproving stare before returning to breakfast.

"Never mind—I didn't think you would. Thanks all the same." Carolyn dodged back to avoid raindrops pelting in the car and, shrugging, rolled the window back up. All she could do was wait for a passing car to offer help. If she stood out on the roadside, she would merely add a thorough soaking to her list of calamitous happenings.

She heard the noise of a heavy engine on the grade behind her and her face brightened. Rolling down the car window again, she leaned out and waved enthusiastically at the driver of a gasoline truck, which was grinding up to the top of the hill.

The solemn, thin-faced man gave her a disapproving stare as the truck pulled slowly past. He looked remarkably like the cow.

"Hey . . . wait!" Carolyn shouted, trying to find

the catch on her door. "I need help. Oh, for pete's sake . . . can't you even stop?" This was said to the back of the truck, which had continued on its way. "Damn!" She pulled her head back in again and rolled up the window in angry jerks. "Some welcome for the poor tourists. The idiot probably thought I was trying to flirt with him."

She felt water running down her neck and took a quick glance at herself in the rear-vision mirror. The fair shoulder-length hair which had been neatly turned under in a loose pageboy style when she left her Bath hotel an hour earlier was now hanging in soggy strands dripping onto the collar of her nylon raincoat. Rain had also washed all the powder from a pert nose and high cheekbones. Fortunately her dark brown brows and lashes were a provident gift from a Celtic ancestor and had been left unscathed by the dampness. At the moment, they provided an effective frame for the angry greenish-hazel eyes which stared back from the mirror.

It was no wonder the truck driver wouldn't stop; she looked like a dispossessed gypsy. Why on earth hadn't she put on a head scarf before hanging out the window. Disconsolately, she reached for a comb and started to repair the damage. In her present condition . . . anything would help.

Another glance at the road confirmed the lack of traffic, wheeled or otherwise. What in the world was the matter with the British, she wondered? At nine o'clock in the morning, the place should be teeming with people. Of course if she hadn't decided to take this scenic drive from Beechen Cliff, the rescue forces might have been more numerous. Obviously very few people chose a scenic drive in the midst of a downpour. And how many would try it on a cold Sunday morning in June? Evidently only an American with more enthusiasm than sense.

Which describes me to a T, Carolyn decided, shrugging down in the driver's seat and resting her head against the leather upholstery. At this rate, she'd never get to Wales. She watched the rain streaming down the windshield and let her eyelids droop down. If she was destined to be stranded, she might as well make herself comfortable. Her bed the night before must have been a legacy from King Bladud, who fed his pigs on acorns in the sixteenth century. During his reign, he had evidently stuffed some of the Bath hotel mattresses with any nuts he had left over. She grinned wearily and fitted her shoulders into the crack between the car seat and the door. After that hotel bed, she needed revitalizing and a small nap might help.

Later on, it took a muffled thumping next to her ear to bring her back to the world of the living. Her eyes flashed open to see a huddled figure pounding on her car window. Still half-asleep, she groped for the window handle and wound the glass down a bare half inch, noting thankfully that the car door was securely locked.

"What do you want?" she managed in as haughty a tone as possible.

"Not what you're evidently thinking," came a disgusted and extremely American voice. "I just stopped because I saw the U.S.A. plate on your bumper and I thought you might be in trouble." His brusque tone made her understand that he was performing a necessary duty to a fellow citizen but frankly his heart wasn't in it.

That discounted any Good Samaritan aspect his action might have possessed as far as Carolyn was concerned. She sat up straighter and wound down the window further to make sure her disdain got across.

"Act-u-al-ly," she drew the word out to four syllables in an assumed British accent, "there is a spot of trouble under the bonnet but there's no need for you to bother."

"That stiff upper lip lingo would be a lot more effective if the corn pone didn't keep slipping through," he said laconically. "Is it Virginia or further south?"

"North Carolina," she admitted, reverting to normal. "About a million years ago."

He pulled a handkerchief from his raincoat pocket and wiped off the water starting to run down his neck. "Could we discuss your family tree after I get in out of the rain?"

She took another wary look at his tall figure. "The hood," she volunteered, "is out there."

"So is the rain. Look, Miss . . ."

"Drummond. Caro . . . I mean, Carolyn Drummond."

"Miss Drummond. I'm Mike Evans and I work in Chicago. I pay my taxes regularly and vote every four years." The rain was putting a wave back in his slicked-down short brown hair. "I'm merely over here on vacation to see the tennis at Wimbledon. My dear sweet old mother lives in Michigan and she taught me to assist unaccompanied ladies with car trouble. I can change a tire or check your spark plugs as soon as you tell me what happened. Beyond that, I haven't the slightest interest in your personal life. Frankly I have a redhead at the moment who keeps me broke but happy. I also haven't had breakfast yet and I never ravish helpless females on an empty stomach. Now—do you want help or shall I cross you off my list?"

Meekly Carolyn reached over and unlocked the passenger door.

"Please get in, Mr. Evans."

"Thank you." He punctuated his acceptance with a mighty sneeze.

The nearest cow stopped chewing her cud long enough to watch him fit his broad shoulders into the pint-sized door opening on the far side.

"My God, what a climate," he said after slamming the door. "It feels more like November than June."

The advent of his long masculine figure in the car's cramped quarters made Carolyn feel that she was practically sitting on his lap. She drew back from his dripping raincoat like a fastidious cat avoiding a wet sidewalk.

"It always rains in England in June," she said, frowning.

"I know," he stowed his handkerchief away and turned to give her a closer look, "but it's all right to gripe about it. It's one of the provisions listed on your airline ticket. Even the natives join in." His blue eyes appraised her mockingly. "The only difference is that they say 'it's shocking ... simply shocking.'"

She was puzzled. "Then why did you come?"

"I told you. I wanted to take in Wimbledon."

"Four thousand miles for a tennis match?"

He shrugged. "We all have our hobbies. I don't drink heavily or chase female tourists." His glance slid over her curved figure casually but appreciatively. "Tennis is cheaper in the long run."

"Very funny." The irritation was beginning to come back. There was no doubt in her mind that Michael Evans with his rugged good looks and calm assurance wouldn't have to chase any woman very far. That formidable jaw line of his meant persistence and she'd seen the firm mouth settle into a line of pure determination. She intercepted a mocking look and felt her cheeks flame. "You did say something about fixing my car."

"So I did." He was searching through his pockets. "Do you have a cigarette?"

"Er ... yes." Momentarily she was diverted and searched in her big purse. Naturally the cigarette package had slid to the bottom and she had to pull out a package of tissues, her passport, a credit card holder, and a coin purse before she unearthed it. "Help yourself."

"Thanks." He took one out and handed it back. "Could I borrow a match too?"

She stopped repacking her purse and started unpacking again. The matches were finally found in a bottom corner. She handed them over and heard him chuckle at the miscellaneous array of articles in her lap. "Would you like anything else?" she asked sweetly, indicating the pile. "Chewing gum for the natives—pills for motion sickness—a currency converter . . ."

"I could use some bacon and eggs."

"Sorry, I'm fresh out." She watched him light the cigarette with an economy of gesture, and stretch long legs out in front of him as far as the scaled-down dimensions of the car would permit. It was like trying to fit a Great Dane in a cat carrier, she decided.

"Since we've completed my biography, it's your turn," he said. "What are you doing in a stalled car all by yourself in the middle of the English countryside?"

14

"Not admiring the view. I'd planned to be admiring the Wales countryside by now but this darned car won't cooperate. The steam started pouring out of the hood on the last hill and after a couple of gasps . . ." she gestured graphically, "poof! It just lay down and died."

"That eliminates being out of gas or a garden-variety flat tire." He rolled down his window to let the cigarette smoke drift outside. "It also means trouble on a Sunday morning."

"I don't understand."

"It sounds like a broken radiator hose to me."

"What's so bad about that? Can't you give me a lift back to Bath? I'd be glad to pay you for a ride to the nearest garage."

"Don't start acting like the kind of tourist we all get blamed for," he broke in irritably when she would have reached for her purse.

"What's wrong with offering to pay for your time and services?"

"You'd better find out first if they're for sale."

She looked at him blankly. "Well?"

"They're not."

"Thanks very much. You don't mind then if I continue trying to hail a truck driver? In the meantime, make yourself comfortable, of course."

"You can climb down off your high horse too," he said with resignation. "I'm not planning to leave you by the roadside."

"What *do* you plan to do?"

"I was merely pointing out that even if I took

you all the way back to London, you couldn't get any spare parts for your engine's innards today. Sunday is Sunday ... especially in England." He ground out his cigarette in the ashtray. "All the garage mechanics are probably sitting around over their second 'cuppa' at breakfast and planning what they'll do at home on a rainy Sunday." He looked bleakly out at the streaming countryside. "I know what I'd do in their place."

Carolyn couldn't throttle her curiosity. "What?"

"Go back to bed." He yawned mightily.

She thought of her hotel mattress in Bath and shuddered. "Could we please get back to my car engine?"

"If you insist." He flicked a brief glance her way. "You have a one-track mind. Why do you want to go to Wales?"

"Not to attend a tennis tournament."

"Vacation?"

"Nope."

"Ancestor worship?"

"Of course not." She glared at him. "And you talk about a one-track mind."

He merely grinned and waited for her to go on.

"I have to go to Wales," she explained grudgingly, "because I'm supposed to buy a castle. It's a little difficult to explain."

He pushed back warily in his seat. "Any special castle? The last I heard Caernarvon and Harlech weren't for sale."

"I know that, and I'm not pricing Buckingham so you can stop looking at me as if I'd just stepped out of a straitjacket. This is sort of a mini-castle called Lyonsgate overlooking the Irish Sea in South Wales."

"Something for roughing it on long weekends, I take it. It's a long way to commute from North Carolina."

"Stop sounding so superior." She ran a hand distractedly through her hair. "Look—the castle isn't for me. Good heavens, I couldn't afford the front door of one but the man I work for doesn't have any budget problems. You've probably heard of Lyon's Furniture. . . ." she watched him nod slowly. "Well, I work for old Henry Lyon who made his first million so long ago that he's forgotten when. Anyhow, after he heard Lyonsgate Castle was for sale, he decided he had to have it."

"What does that have to do with you?"

"Liz Sheppard and I are his secretaries. He knew that we were planning a vacation over here so he decided we might as well have a working holiday. Three weeks off at full salary after we spend a week in Wales determining if the castle's a good buy. He said he'll take our word for it."

"Aren't you a little young for decisions like that?"

"I'm twenty-five," she replied, stung by his insinuation.

"Ummm . . . you look more like nineteen," he

17

informed her, and then grinned at her outraged reaction. "Simmer down. When you reach my advanced age of thirty-five—that's a compliment."

"Are you really? Thirty-five, I mean." It was her turn to stare. "You don't look it."

"Thanks very much. I have a few years yet before I apply for social security, so you needn't be too concerned."

"I didn't mean it that way. . . ."

Her discomfiture didn't faze him. "Forget it. Are you on a tight schedule for this venture of yours?"

She nodded unhappily. "I'm supposed to be at Lyon tomorrow. Liz wrote to the caretaker and made the arrangements."

"Why can't . . . Liz . . . deputize for you?"

"Because she's up in Scotland on another commission for old Henry right now."

Mike absently cleared the steam from his side window. "Not another castle?"

"Of course not," Caro snapped. "There are some paintings to be auctioned and Mr. Lyon wanted her to put in a bid. She's to join me at the castle later in the week. By that time, I would have completed the preliminary survey. But now this miserable car has decided to stop running." She turned an earnest face to him. "Are you sure English mechanics don't work on Sunday?"

"Practically positive."

"Then what are my chances of a car rental?"

He shrugged. "About the same as getting a mechanic today."

"Well, you needn't sound so complacent about it," she snapped in desperation. "Surely there's a train running if you could drop me off at a station." She gave him a careful look. "Unless, of course, you might be headed toward Wales. Are you, Mr. Evans?"

The glance that met hers was equally thoughtful. "I suppose I could," he answered as if thinking aloud. "I have a few days to spare before Wimbledon gets underway."

Her eyes gleamed with excitement. "That's marvelous! I'll be glad to pay whatever you ask."

"Don't be so damned rash," he cautioned. "You're practically begging me to fleece you."

She waved this aside. "You don't look the type. Besides, Mr. Lyon is very generous and once he hears how you've rescued me, he'll probably write a whopping check."

"Let's wait and see." He started to open the door. "Give me your keys and I'll transfer your luggage."

She handed them over. "There are just two bags. I'll carry these maps and guidebooks."

He took a last look around. "Okay—then go back and get in my car." He nodded behind them. "I'll leave your keys in the glove compartment, so the garage man can find them."

"Hey, wait a minute," she protested as he started back to the trunk. "Hadn't you better take a quick look inside the hood before I give up completely on this car? After all, it might be something simple."

"All right . . . I'll look," he agreed impatiently, pulling up his raincoat collar against the sudden gusts. "You can get moved to my bus in the meantime. I think we've held down this part of the English countryside long enough."

Carolyn's mouth dropped slightly open in surprise and she stared as he moved off. It was a little premature for Michael Evans to be issuing orders. Evidently he believed in taking over with a vengeance. Somewhat distractedly she fumbled for the maps on the back seat of the car. Out of the corner of her eye, she saw the hood of the car go up and then a few minutes later, it was slammed down. She peered through the windshield and intercepted his clear-cut signal of a thumb jerked back toward his car.

Sighing slightly, she gathered the rest of her belongings and prepared to evacuate. Perhaps she had been a little precipitate in trusting him. After all, what did she know about the man other than that he was a tennis fan and harbored a redheaded girlfriend back home. She paused with her hand on the door handle and peered through the glass at the deserted countryside.

At the moment, it was a choice between Mike Evans or the herd of cows beyond the hedgerow. She hesitated no longer. It was definitely better to have a two-footed friend than a crowd of four-footed ones under present circumstances. Huddling down into her raincoat like a turtle pulling back into its shell, she made a dash toward the neat blue sedan parked tidily on the shoulder behind her.

The transfer was effected in less time than she had thought possible. Just minutes later Mike was pulling out onto the hard surface of the road and she was bestowing a nostalgic glance on her deserted car.

"Don't worry," he said, intercepting it. "I'll call from the nearest phone box and have the garage people tow it back to Bath."

"Was it trouble with the radiator?"

"Your hose looked like a piece of cheesecloth," he confirmed. "It may take a while to get a replacement."

"So much for my luck with foreign cars," she said morosely. Looking around the pale blue interior of his Vauxhall, she added, "This doesn't seem like your type either."

"What type am I . . . Bentley, Jaguar, or Morris Minor?"

"I'll let you know when I decide," she said, sitting back. "Be sure and keep track of your mileage for your expense account and if you'd like help with the driving, I'll be glad to spell you." She hesitated and then confessed, "Being on the wrong side of the road doesn't confuse me, but sometimes I have to circle the roundabouts more than once to find the proper exit."

He shuddered visibly. "I'll manage the driving."

"I'm not that bad. . . ."

"I didn't say you were," he pointed out reasonably.

"It wasn't what you said," she commented dryly. "It was that wince of pain."

"You're overly sensitive. No one could blame you for the condition of that radiator hose. It's fortunate that you got as far as Bath."

"It wasn't any great accomplishment," she told him. "I just picked the car up there yesterday after I came from London on the train." She glanced across at his intent profile. "Where have you been?"

"Before Bath, you mean?" He was concentrating on passing two very wet teen-agers on motor bikes. "My last stop was Hampton Court Palace."

"That tremendous grape vine there is almost unbelievable, isn't it?" When he didn't answer, she repeated her question.

He shifted uneasily and took his time before saying, "Well, actually I can't tell you. I spent my time checking the dimensions of the Tudor Tennis Court at the back of the Palace."

"For heaven's sake—why?"

"I wondered whether King Henry VII laid out a regulation-sized court."

Caro was horrified. "You mean you didn't see any of the paintings?"

His jaw jutted stubbornly. "Now look . . .

King Henry VIII was supposed to have been playing tennis in 1536 when Anne Boleyn was beheaded."

"Big deal." She refused to be pacified. "You didn't even go down and look at those fantastic serving kitchens?"

"Charles the First was playing on those courts the same day he made his escape."

"And you missed the Christopher Wren additions to the Palace?'

"But I learned that the Earl of Essex swatted the Prince of Wales with his racquet about 1630. Must have been after a bad call by a linesman."

"I give up," Carolyn said flatly.

"Good! I thought you might." He shot her an amused glance. "Stop trying to reform me."

"You're a barbarian."

"Very possibly." He lowered his speed to go around one of the many circles that British highway engineers have lavishly spread over their roads as safety features rather than intersections.

"Although they're not . . . you know," Carolyn continued.

"Not what?"

"Safer than intersections," she said, giving voice to her thoughts. "These roundabouts, I mean."

"I thought you were still dwelling on my savage ancestry."

She shook her head. "I gave up on that. Besides, it's your vacation. I suppose looking at tennis courts isn't any worse than touring gardens or visiting cathedrals."

The laughter lines around his eyes deepened. "That's big of you. All things considered, tennis nuts are a pretty harmless bunch compared to other people. I was on a ship full of bridge players once when they announced that Fiji was visible on the port side. The woman next to me didn't even look up—she just bid three no trump."

"Did she make it?" Carolyn broke out laughing at his affronted look. "I'm just kidding."

"So was I. Incidentally, I did see Hampton Court properly some years ago, so you can stop trying to save my soul."

"Your soul is of no concern to me," she said loftily.

"That's a pity—maybe it will grow on you. Meanwhile, take a gander at those maps beside you and see if you can find where this road intersects the M-4 motorway. We should have run into it by now."

After a few minutes' search, Carolyn could tell him explicitly why they had not run into the M-4. "You should have angled right when we were on the last roundabout. No—don't turn back," she added hastily as he started to pull off on the shoulder. "There's another chance at it a few miles on."

He obediently turned back on the road. "I hope you're right. How can they hide anything as big as the Severn Bridge? It marks the boundary of Wales."

"Highway engineers can hide anything. Or haven't you ever tried to find an entrance to the Triborough Bridge?"

"As seldom as possible. I miss it oftener than I find it." He rubbed the steamy windshield with the back of his hand. "This damned rain doesn't look as if it's going to stop for a month."

"At least a month," she agreed. "I should have told Mr. Lyon that I'd look at his castle in August." She shivered inside her raincoat. "Right now I feel as if I've crawled inside an oyster. My hotel room felt like one last night too." She heard his deep chuckle and he started to hum softly. "Okay, I give up," she said finally, "what's the name of that tune?"

"It's an old one about the oyster and the restaurant." Obligingly he sang the lyric in a pleasant baritone:

"The oyster wept a bitter tear saying 'I've been in forty-seven stews since eight o'clock tonight— for I'm the only oyster working here!' "

The last line ended in wild harmony as Carolyn joined him on the last two words.

"Bravo!" he applauded. "Let's try it again."

"Not on your life. From now on, we'll pay attention to the road signs and turn toward Wales. If I get involved in a concert, heaven knows where we'll end up."

His eyes were still alight with laughter. "You're probably right. All right, Miss Drummond—we'll play it your way for a while."

"And then?"

"Let's decide later." He pointed toward an entrance to the busy motorway ahead of them. "What do you know—we made it. Wales, here we come."

"Ready or not." She leaned forward, peering through the windshield.

"It reminds me of that English king," he mused.

"Which English king?"

"Ethelred the Unready. I always thought it was a wonderful name. He came to the throne in 978."

Her mouth dropped open and then snapped shut as he turned a bland glance toward her.

"Something wrong?" he asked.

"I'm not sure. First, you're a tennis fanatic—then a connoisseur of vaudeville songs—now a name-dropper in English history." Her eyes narrowed in suspicion. "Maybe I should have stayed by the side of the road, Mr. Evans."

"Perfectly harmless, I assure you, Miss Drummond."

"For a minute, I thought one of the nuts had rolled out of my mattress."

"We obviously stayed at the same hotel in Bath. No wonder you're on edge. Lean back and rest for a while."

She obeyed reluctantly. "Wake me when we get to Wales."

"You prefer the direct route?"

She opened one eye. "Absolutely."

He sighed. "Coward."

"You bet." She closed the eye decisively. After a minute she heard him start to hum and she relaxed in a haze of contentment. For such an aggravating man, Michael Evans was astonishingly comfortable to have along.

Chapter Two

It was some time later that Carolyn felt a gentle nudge and then heard Mike announcing in his best tour-guide tones: "We are now approaching Cymru by way of the famous Severn Bridge."

She kept her eyes deliberately closed. "Three no trump."

"Don't try that on me." The next nudge wasn't gentle. "Sit up and look around."

"You needn't bruise me for life," she complained mildly as she obeyed. "What the dickens is Cymru?"

"Cymru, Miss Drummond, is the Welsh name for Wales."

"Oh, for pete's sake. . . ."

"You," he pointed out, "were the one bemoaning my lack of culture." He edged over to the slower lane of the motorway. "Feast your eyes on the countryside. There's quite a view from the bridge."

Carolyn stared with fascination at the gently rolling tablelands in front of her. Below the huge suspension bridge, the broad mouth of the Severn river coiled lazily toward Bridgwater Bay and eventually out into the busy Bristol Channel. The gray of the slow-moving water reflected the overcast sky but nothing could have dulled the brilliant green of the land in front of them.

Prickly hedgerows neatly bisected hillsides still thickly dotted with trees, and fat sheep and cattle grazed contentedly in the lush pasture grass. To the north, a partial arc of rainbow sliced through the clouds and stabbed into earth beside a clump of sturdy oaks.

"Like a lifeline thrown down from heaven," Carolyn said in a hushed voice, "and the countryside is so beautiful that the rainbow fits right in."

"I thought you'd like it. Apparently the natives do too. They were taken into the English fold in 1536, but they're still a stubborn Celtic lot. Up the border a bit, there's a ditch called Offa's Dyke dating from the eighth century which was dug just to keep the Anglo-Saxons separate from the Welsh. It's there today and neither side has suggested filling it in. A lot of Welsh nationalists still insist on speaking their old tongue too."

Caro groaned. "Oh lord, all those double D's

and double L's. I had trouble enough with just plain English in London."

"I know. I had to ask the same directions three times yesterday before I could find a person who could understand my accent. Look out!" He swerved suddenly to avoid a bubble-topped mini-car that cut recklessly in front of them. "Damn! Drivers are the same the world over." He let his speed edge up again. "The two great international games are 'Crinkle Fender' and 'Run the Stoplight.'"

"Cynic."

"You're right. Take a quick look at the map and see if we take this next exit for Chepstow."

She rummaged on the seat beside her before saying, "It looks like it—if it's spelled the way it's pronounced. What's at Chepstow?"

"Lunch." Mike pulled into the slow lane for the exit. "If your heart desires more, the guidebook says there's a castle as well. It will give you practice on inspecting them."

"You don't have to convince me with castles." She delved into her purse looking for a comb and mirror. "I'm starving—breakfast was a long time ago."

"There's even a break in the weather. Maybe we can eat lunch without getting drenched."

Her comb stopped by her ear. "Why should we get drenched eating in a restaurant?"

He maneuvered in and out of a roundabout, turning onto a narrow, twisting road before he answered. "We're not eating in a restaurant. I had the hotel furnish a hamper before I left Bath. There should be plenty for both of us." He caught her dubious look. "I'll be glad to take you to a restaurant if you'd rather. That is, if there *is* a restaurant that's open on Sunday. Between the weekends, holidays, and early closing days in the villages, a man can starve to death in this part of the world. Ireland's even worse," he continued darkly. "They roll up the sidewalks on race days as well."

She noted his broad shoulders. "It doesn't look as if you're on the brink of starvation."

He grinned. "Forewarned is forearmed. I remember a Yugoslavian train where we were without a dining car for twenty-four hours."

"What did you do?" she asked, interested in spite of herself.

"Fortunately there was a blonde in the next compartment who rescued me."

"I thought you liked redheads," she said dryly.

"Not when the blonde has a hamper full of sliced chicken, cheese, and red wine."

"I should have known. Didn't the language give you any trouble?"

"Not that you'd notice." There was a decided twinkle in the look he directed her way. "She worked in the American embassy in Belgrade."

"Men!"

"Well, don't get mad," he said reasonably.

"This time I'm offering to share my lunch with you, so it all works out."

She yanked the comb through her hair so hard that it brought tears to her eyes. Obviously he was right. There was no real reason to be irritated, but there was a maddening imperturbability about the man beside her; enough to make the sparks fly from any female.

Carolyn swallowed hard and decided she would bide her time. "I'll be glad to accept," she said finally.

"Was it so hard?" He was definitely amused now.

"Certainly not. Tell me about your redhead."

He slowed to let a delivery van turn off the road. "Which one?"

"The one at home who keeps you broke and happy."

"Oh—*that* one. You mean Gina."

"Do I?" She closed her purse with a decided snap. "What's she like?"

He thought for a minute. Then slowly: "Well, she's sleek—marvelous lines. Wonderful to be with . . . you know Italians. . . ."

With a vivid mental picture of a bosomy European actress, Carolyn hastily sought another subject. "Do you have the same interests?"

"Maybe. Who cares? When I'm around her, I don't stop to think. But one of these days," he promised solemnly, "we'll take time out to talk."

"Oh really . . ." She flounced on the seat.

"Male conceit never ceases to amaze me. The feeling that any woman can be had—" She broke off abruptly and reached down at her side for the guidebook. "You don't mind if I read about Chepstow?" she asked in saccharine accents.

"Certainly not."

She made a show of flipping the pages. "Some of us ... some women, I mean, do have other things on our minds. . . ."

"Other than what?"

"Other than se ..." She clamped down hurriedly as her trend of thought became vocal. "Other than the lighter things of life," she finished lamely. There came a noise suspiciously like a snort from her side but she kept her eyes glued to the guidebook. "Did you know that Chepstow Castle underwent two sieges in the civil wars of the seventeenth century?"

"If we're being honest, I haven't lost a wink of sleep over the civil wars of the seventeenth century," he assured her.

She looked up as he maneuvered through an ancient town gate and then checked her book again. "It even tells about this," she said triumphantly before reading from the text. "The main road passes through a town gate, where, from the fourteenth century, traders bringing goods and cattle had to pay a due to their lord."

"Uh-huh." He let the car idle past deserted doorways. "I'll be damned—"

"What now?"

34

"Everything's closed. Just as I suspected."

"There *are* more important things than eating lunch," she pointed out with some asperity. "You should be appreciating the lines of the castle on the hillside. This book says it was built soon after the Conquest."

"Now look, my prickly friend ... each to his own. Just because we're sharing the same car doesn't mean that I apologize each time you sneeze. I'm well aware of Chepstow Castle and its history. But at the moment, I'm a hell of a lot more interested in finding a telephone and a place where we can eat in comfort."

His calm rebuke made Carolyn feel about three inches tall. "I'm sorry," she stammered at length, "I suppose I deserved that. Old Henry keeps me whittled down to size most of the time."

"Most employers do."

"I'm his goddaughter as well, so that gives him freer rein. Liz shrinks any swelled heads the rest of the time."

"Poor Carolyn," he mocked gently.

"Not really." She wondered when he had decided to go on a first-name basis. "I haven't suffered at all. Why do you need a telephone?"

"To call a garage in Bath. For your car ... remember?"

"Of course." She pushed her fingers through her hair in some confusion and tried again. "There's a hotel over there. It must be open on Sundays."

"I think you're right." He indicated a wooded patch over to their left. "The castle grounds are over there just a couple blocks. I'll park the car close by and let you look around while I telephone. You can pick out a good place to eat lunch."

"How your mind dwells on that topic," she murmured wickedly.

He merely grinned and turned onto a side road. "Don't disturb the driver. It's hard enough to remember to stick to the left side of the road on the straightaway, but at their intersections it's doubly bad."

"I know. There's a terrible tendency to climb the curb when a car approaches, too." She looked around with interest as he pulled into a cleared space marked "Car Park" and stopped under a leafy elm tree at the back. "This is nice and it's practically deserted. Chepstow can't be on the tour bus route."

"Don't you believe it." He got out of the car and stretched. "They'll be along shortly." He nodded toward the stone monument above them. "Can you imagine a castle without a tourist?"

Carolyn got out on her side of the car and looked at the well-ventilated remains on the hill. "I don't know," she said dubiously. "That one looks pretty moth-eaten."

"So would you if you'd been around since the Norman Conquest," he informed her. "I'll go along and find a telephone. Will you be all right?"

"Of course." She waved toward the deserted delivery van parked next to them. "Evidently only the ghosts are stirring today."

"Don't you believe it." Mike shrugged out of his raincoat and threw it on the front seat. "Wait until we unpack the lunch. The visitors will start crawling out of the tree trunks."

"Go make your telephone call. I'll absorb all the cultural facts while you're gone."

"Just so you don't absorb . . ."

"The lunch?" she interrupted. "Scout's honor, I won't go near the hamper—but you *do* have a fixation on the subject."

"I wasn't referring to food that time," he corrected with a slow smile. "Don't go sitting on the grass around here. It's still damp from the showers."

"Yes, sir," she curtsied obediently, "very good, sir."

"My God," he said half-seriously, "what have I gotten into? I may be a while getting back," he threatened, "if the hotel bar is open. I'm beginning to think I need fortifying."

"Do that," she said amiably, "but if you're too long, I'll come hunting for you and peer mournfully over the swinging door."

His eyes sparkled. "I'll bet you would, too. All right, I'll hurry. Don't take up with the castle ghosts while I'm away."

She waved casually and watched him disappear up the lane.

Before leaving the car, she cast an undecided glance at the raincoat he had dropped on the seat. Since she couldn't lock the doors, perhaps it would be wiser to stash it in the bottom of the car where it wouldn't be such a temptation. "Although the British would resent my slur on their honesty," she muttered, picking up the coat and starting to fold the sleeves. A glimpse of the label from a famous New York men's store confirmed the quality and her suspicion of its worth—just as his brown, houndstooth-check sport coat proclaimed itself cashmere and his plain-cut beige slacks meant fine flannel.

Michael Evans' assured and forceful manner went right along with his well-chosen clothes, but the man surely wasn't the innocuous tourist or hobbyist he was pretending to be. On the other hand, how could anyone else interrupt his schedule to make a side trip involving hundreds of miles.

She would stake her traveler's checks that he had been inwardly laughing at her when she quoted a rate for renting his car ... despite his solemn expression. It was, she decided thoughtfully, a little like having a chauffeur who combined the muscles of a cowboy star and the diplomacy of the British prime minister.

She put the raincoat in a neat bundle on the floor by the back seat and then stared down at her own wrinkled coat in discouragement. The way she looked at the moment, she couldn't attract any man even if he didn't have a luscious Italian import waiting in the United States. She scrubbed futilely at a small grease mark on her raincoat hem and tried to straighten her chartreuse knit skirt. While the suit fulfilled the manufacturer's promises about permanent press and soil resistance, it also had an unfortunate tendency to look like a junior high gym tunic.

Her shopping spree in London's Bond Street had been postponed due to a tight schedule and now Carolyn found herself bitterly resenting it. It would be nice to look provocative and decorative instead of neat and dull. She gave herself a stiff mental shake and slammed the car door. At this rate, she'd be needing hot milk at night to go to sleep. The thing to do was to drive directly to Lyonsgate Castle, write Michael Evans a check, and calmly send him on his way. "And don't forget it," she told herself sternly.

A sudden breeze ruffled the leaves in the tree above her and she glanced up curiously. There was still blue sky overhead, although gray clouds lingered stubbornly on the periphery. Their picnic lunch might be a reality, after all, she decided.

She dug into her pocket for her guidebook and leafed through it until she came to the part on Chepstow. If she read the history of the ruined castle, it would make her tour more interesting.

Deep in the details of a siege on the castle in 1645, she was scarcely aware of the footsteps on the gravel nearby until she heard a sharp wrench of metal and some fluent cursing in a foreign tongue. She looked up to find a thickset man with a worn cap on his head wrenching irritably at the door of the delivery van next to Mike's car. The catch on the door finally gave way and Carolyn started to resume her interrupted reading when she noticed a piece of paper flutter to the ground as the man climbed into the driver's seat of the van.

For a moment she hesitated, frowning. Then with some reluctance she marked her place in the guidebook and started over to pick up the paper so she could restore it to the driver.

She stooped to retrieve the white scrap skittering playfully in the breeze and turned toward the van. The driver was in the process of starting his engine and didn't see her until their eyes met in his side mirror. Carolyn's friendly manner crumbled as she encountered that malevolent glare and heard him gun the accelerator impatiently.

"Just a minute—this belongs to you," she said, hurrying up alongside. She waved the paper in explanation and waited for him to open the door, when he suddenly gunned the motor again and started to drive off. "Hey! You forgot . . . oh, look out!" Her hail turned to a cry of pain as the rear fender scraped her thigh and hip—throwing her to the ground as she tried to get out of the way.

She had a confused glimpse of the driver's determined face and the flash of a gray-haired man sitting in the passenger's seat before the truck screeched onto the main street and disappeared in a haze of dirty exhaust.

The sudden shock and the painful smarting of her leg kept her sprawled motionless for a minute. She was just struggling to her feet when Michael caught sight of her on his return from the hotel. He took the last half block at a dead run and was breathing hard when he pounded up beside her.

"For God's sake, Carolyn ... what happened? Are you all right?" His bewildered gaze took in her dirty coat and the ruined stocking now streaked with blood. He half led, half carried her back to the car where he lowered her gently on the front seat. Taking another look at her cornstarch complexion, he immediately shoved her head down over her knees. "Don't faint on me! Not now ..."

Her world stopped whirling in a minute or so and she gingerly sat up, only to lean back against the seat.

"Why not?" she managed with a vestige of humor. "Don't English doctors work on Sunday either?"

"We'll soon find out."

"No ... Mr. Evans ... Mike ... please don't!"

41

She put out a restraining hand as he would have moved around to the driver's seat. "Other than ruining a stocking, I'm perfectly fine." Her eyes dropped under his dubious look. "Maybe black and blue in some unmentionable places but . . ."

"More than that, I think." He gestured toward the blood on her leg.

"It's just a nick from the zipper on my raincoat lining when the fender caught me. Honestly, I mean it," she pleaded as his expression remained unconvinced. "All I need is to wash and change clothes."

"I suppose you can do that up at the hotel," he said slowly.

"Well, then—that's settled." She started to get out of the car.

"Hold it." Firmly he pushed her back. "Nothing's settled. How did you come to tangle with that truck fender in the first place?"

"It was the darndest thing." She became aware that she was still clutching the piece of paper and smoothed it on her lap. "Here's the real culprit?"

"What is it?"

"I don't know. It fluttered down when the driver started to get in the truck. I thought it might be important so I tried to return it to him." She shook her head ruefully. "My lord, you'd have thought I was stalking him with a hand grenade. He took one look at me and floored the accelerator. It's a good thing I wasn't in front of him because I suspect he would have reacted just the same way."

"Well, take it easy. It's all over now." He moved closer. "Let's take a look at the paper. Maybe that will help explain it."

"Here—you hold it. My hands are still shaky."

Obediently he took it and then frowned as he read it. "It's only an invoice for some cheese."

"Cheese!"

He nodded. "The letterhead is from the London branch of Wellington Foods Ltd. They're billing somebody for six crates of New Zealand cheddar." He turned the paper over and scanned the back. "S'funny—there's no consignee listed."

"Very funny! Why would anybody run me down because of that thing?"

"I can't imagine. Was there any advertising painted on the panel of the truck?"

"I'm sure there wasn't. Don't you remember—it was pretty shabby-looking. And the man who climbed in wasn't wearing a delivery uniform, either." She shook her head in disgust. "What a way for me to go ... flattened under a load of cheese!"

"If it makes you feel any better, New Zealanders think highly of their cheddar," he said with the shadow of a smile. "Move over so I can close the door."

"What now?"

"I'll drive you up to the hotel so you can change." He slid onto the seat and put the key in the ignition. "While we're there, I'll try and call the Wellington Foods office and see why their drivers are careering around the Welsh countryside." He glanced hopefully at her. "You didn't get the license number?"

She shook her head. "Sorry. It didn't enter my mind and there must be hundreds of trucks like that on the road, so there'll be no use phoning the police. I couldn't even tell them the make."

"Damn! I suppose you're right," he added grudgingly as the car drew up before a rather dingy, brick-fronted building. "Are you sure you feel like driving on after you change?"

"Honestly, I'll be fine once I scrape off this grime. If you'll get my small bag out of the trunk, I can be ready for lunch in fifteen minutes. And *that* should make you feel better," she said mischievously.

For once, he didn't respond. "Believe it or not, I've lost my appetite."

"That doesn't make sense. I get hit and you're suffering from shock."

A slow smile finally emerged. "You're getting back to normal mighty fast," he said reprovingly. "C'mon around to the trunk while I get the bag. Then we'll ask the desk clerk if you can wash your dirty face."

Half an hour later, a very different-looking Carolyn emerged, having changed into dark green knit slacks and a striped boxy jacket of the same material.

"The pants hide the battle scars and band-aids," she explained to Mike as she met him in the lobby of the hotel. "This way I won't disgrace you."

"I wasn't worried," he drawled. As they went out to the car, he noted her slight limp. "Does it hurt to walk?"

"Hardly at all. Where do we have our picnic?"

He put her suitcase in the trunk and slammed the lid before answering. "You can pick the view, but I think we'd better sit in the car. Some springs and padding might help."

She nodded and let herself into the front seat carefully. "Let's drive on until we find some different scenery. Frankly, I'd just as soon forget Chepstow Castle."

It was on a wide spot in the road by the meandering river Wye with gentle green hills on either side that they finally delved into the picnic basket.

"I hope you like cheese and tomato sandwiches," Mike told her, handing a packet across, "since they're the only kind we have."

"I do I've had a dozen already on this trip." Carolyn took a hungry bite. "Cheese and tomato sandwiches are to England as cheeseburgers are to the U.S.A."

"Wales, my girl. England stopped at the Severn Bridge."

"Maybe that's why the man tried to run me

45

down," she quipped. "Some welcome to the country, I must say."

"We won't know for a while. There wasn't any answer when I called the Wellington Foods number while you were changing. I'll call again from Swansea tomorrow. Monday morning should find somebody in the office."

She tucked a piece of cheese back in the thinly sliced bread. "I wish I thought it would do some good but frankly . . ." her voice trailed off.

"I know. Well, we'll give it a try, anyhow." He reached for another sandwich half. "At least I arranged to have your car rescued in Bath. I meant to tell you before but all the fracas distracted me."

"Will they tow it back to town?"

He nodded. "And store it after the repair. I have the name of the garage—I'll give it to you later."

"Fine. Any hope for coffee?" She peered in the hamper.

"Sorry, we only run to ginger beer." He grinned at her disappointed face and then relented. Never mind—we'll stop at some place down the road and get something hot."

"Okay." She looked at her watch. "I suppose we shouldn't waste much time if we're to get to Swansea before dark. Is that where we spend the night?"

"I hope to. The desk clerk at Chepstow told me there was a good hotel there." He used a paper napkin and stored it back in the basket with the picnic remains. "You're entitled to an innerspring mattress tonight. Even if it means dispensing with some Olde World charm."

"Hallelujah! I've had enough 'Bed and Breakfasts' in unheated front parlors to last my entire vacation. Let's hope for central heating ... some hot water ..."

"A pile of clean towels ..."

"And a bed lamp bright enough to read by."

"You *are* an optimist," he told her. "I'll settle for any one of those."

"Think positive thoughts and I'll keep my fingers crossed," Carolyn promised solemnly, "for the rest of the afternoon."

Dusk was settling on the hills by the time Mike drove into the outskirts of Wales' second largest city. The lights of Swansea were already flickering in shop windows and over the acres of identical stone row houses favored by the city's inhabitants.

"How do people ever tell which house is theirs?" Carolyn asked, craning her neck to peer up the twisting streets. "The only difference I can see is that some mail slots in the doors are horizontal and some are vertical."

"These were all rebuilt after World War II bombings, so they must like them that way."

"I suppose so," she replied thoughtfully. "If I lived in one, I'd paint stripes on my front door or something."

"Nonconformist!"

She smiled. "Not really, but frankly I'm too tired to argue about it tonight."

"Well, we're almost there." He edged into the outer lane of traffic in the big circle near the center of town. "That's the hotel ahead of us."

"The big modern building? Ummm—I like the looks of it." She started gathering her belongings. "I think we lucked one in."

A uniformed doorman in a resplendent red outfit opened the car doors for them as Mike pulled up in the busy entranceway.

"Good evening, sir. Would you be wanting me to put this in the car park?" His words came out in a measured rhythmic lilt.

"Eventually," Mike replied. "Let me get the bags out of the trunk first."

"Were you planning to spend the night with us, sir?"

Carolyn listened in fascination to the phrasing of his words.

"Yes, of course." Mike paused by the car door. "Is there any difficulty?"

The doorman scratched his head. "Mind you, sir—we're running a bit full tonight. Would you be checking at the desk to see if there's accommodation before I transfer the luggage?"

"Of course." Mike leaned back in the car and whispered to Caro. "Keep those fingers crossed, will you?"

"Absolutely. Tell them we'll take anything—

even a couple of broom closets . . ." She broke off as a noisy group went by on the sidewalk. "Preferably two quiet broom closets."

He merely grinned and said, "Wish me luck" before striding into the lobby.

It was quite a while before he returned. In the interval, Carolyn discovered that she was beginning to ache in every muscle. It would be wonderful to luxuriate in a lovely hot bath, she decided, and was dreaming hopefully when Mike came back to the car and beckoned to the doorman.

She craned her head out the window. "Are we in luck?"

"We're in luck." He waggled a hotel key reassuringly and then gave the car keys to the doorman along with some instructions.

Carolyn got out and went over to wait by the front door. She looked up with a relieved smile as Mike took her elbow and steered her into the building. "You're wonderful," she told him. "It would have been the final blow if they hadn't any rooms."

He paused by the self-service elevators and pushed the button before saying slowly, "The final blow is yet to come."

"Oh oh—let me have it gently." She searched his face. "Are the broom closets located over the jukebox in the bar?"

"They were all out of broom closets." He opened the elevator door, pushed back a protective grill, and motioned her ahead of him.

"But you have a key." Her eyes widened suddenly and she repeated her words. "A key ... only one."

He nodded and held it out before pushing the button for their floor. "Relax—there's lots of space and the clerk assured me we wouldn't be disturbed. That was one of your requirements," he added pointedly.

The grinding noise of the elevator as it took them upward didn't penetrate Carolyn's consciousness at all. Almost as if hypnotized, she concentrated on that brass key dangling from his strong fingers.

"All right." She had difficulty getting the words out. "What kind of a room is it?"

"The best one in the house—that's what the room clerk said. He has a brother in Baltimore, by the way."

"I'm fascinated. What kind of a room?" She went back to the subject relentlessly.

The elevator stopped with a jerk and Michael swept the grilled door open before he replied. "One thing about travel—it's so broadening." His voice was bland. "Tonight, Miss Drummond, we're bedding down in the Bridal Suite." His grin appeared as her mouth dropped open in horror. "Now, watch your step getting out of the elevator or I really *will* have to carry you across the threshold."

Chapter Three

Despite the initial shock, Carolyn found that her evening in the bridal suite would have been approved by a board of church deacons.

Michael had explained the circumstances while he was unlocking the door. "The hotel understands our situation. . . ."

"I'm glad of that," Carolyn said sarcastically. "They can explain it to me. Bridal suites aren't on my tour sheet, Mr. Evans. They frowned on it in my home town."

"We don't schedule orgies in my home town, either." He pushed the door open and motioned her inside. "This," he made an expansive gesture toward the pleasantly furnished living room in front of them, "is a little different. The clerk said there's a lock on the bedroom door. . . ." He led the way into an opulent gold and white bedroom featuring a mammoth double bed draped with a satin spread.

They discreetly moved toward another open door which proved to be a tiled bath done in green and gold.

"We'll take turns with the facilities," Mike went on briskly, "then you lock the bedroom door and I sleep on the couch in the sitting room."

"Well, I suppose it's all right. . . ."

"The room clerk also said there probably wasn't another hotel room in town." Mike scratched the top of his nose thoughtfully. "Of course, we could look for one of those 'Bed and Breakfast' places. . . ."

She shuddered. "No thanks. I'll stay here." Then she frowned again and asked, "How did you register for all this?"

"Not the way you're imagining." He raised a reproving eyebrow. "I put down our own names and the clerk put two different room numbers after them. They probably work this dodge with the suite every time they're full."

"Uh huh . . ."

He cleared his throat. "I did mention that we were cousins. . . ."

This time her eyebrows went up and he went on hurriedly, "I didn't say what kind of cousins."

"That was thoughtful of you."

"Now listen . . ." Evidently he'd reached the end of his tether. "You try having the bridal suite sprung on you sometime. Maybe you'll come up with better answers."

Carolyn smiled then and sank down on the wide couch which faced a paneled fireplace front. "Just call you Ethelred the Unready."

"In spades." He perched on the arm of the couch. "As soon as our bags come up and the housekeeping department brings some bedding for this—we'd better get down to the dining room. These places don't keep late hours."

"Lord yes—don't let's miss dinner." She stood up again with some difficulty. "That cheese and tomato sandwich wore off ages ago. I'll get cleaned up."

He watched her limp toward the bedroom door. "Do you feel like going down? Maybe I can arrange room service."

She looked back, shaking her head. "Not on your life. This is the social event of my day." She gestured toward a wide window with a panoramic city view. "Sunday night in Swansea looks a little quiet."

"There's always the BBC on the tube." He indicated the television set in the corner. "On Sundays, maybe there's a panel discussion on organic gardening."

"I can hardly wait. At least the set looks brand new."

"When would they use it?" His lips quirked with amusement. "In this suite, I mean."

"I know what you mean." Carolyn felt a flush

cover her cheeks and left the room hurriedly on the pretense of wanting to wash her face.

Their evening went as planned.

After the final television program which featured a review of modern poetry and had them both yawning, Carolyn made up Mike's bed on the couch while he took his turn in the bath.

Later, as she prepared for bed, she noted casually that there was neither lock nor key on the bedroom door despite his proclamation to the contrary. Then she remembered the stiff formality with which he had bid her good night and smiled ruefully. He couldn't have made it more apparent that he preferred absent redheaded Italians to bone-weary American blondes.

Her whimsical glance changed to a stony one for no reason at all. There was no reason either for the force she used in punching her pillow into a comfortable position. Even when it was arranged properly, it took a long time before she could finally get to sleep in the quiet room and in that huge bed.

She was awakened the next morning by the ringing of the bedside telephone and a cheerful Welsh voice proclaiming it was eight o'clock plus a very good morning.

When she sleepily agreed and fumbled the receiver back down, pushing an ashtray off the table in the process, she heard a crisp knock on the bedroom door.

"Come in," she called irritably. By that time

54

she was hanging down over the side of the bed and groping for the ashtray.

"Good morning." Mike sounded cheerful, too. "What are you doing down there?"

She raised a flushed countenance. "I always start the day by standing on my head."

His amused glance took in the ashtray clutched in her hand. "Do you mind starting this one about fifteen minutes from now? That's when breakfast is due to arrive. I'll go in and shave first, if that's all right."

"Be my guest," she said, pulling the covers up to her chin and wishing she could pull them over her head. If she'd had any sense, she would have combed her hair before receiving visitors. Even unshaven, Mike looked neat and unperturbed in a dark blue robe covering lighter blue pajamas. His brown hair was already slicked back.

"Thanks. I won't be long." He gave her bed a wide margin as he went by. "We can eat out in the other room if you'll let the waiter in. Don't worry about the bedding—I've put it away." The bathroom door was shut carefully and firmly behind him before she could think of an answer.

When they were in the middle of breakfast, Carolyn asked if they could spend the forenoon in Swansea before driving on to Lyonsgate.

"I'd like to get my hair done," she said plaintively. "After that rainstorm yesterday, it needs refurbishing." Actually, she was still smarting about the way she had looked when he marched through the bedroom earlier.

He glanced up from boiled eggs long enough to inspect the soft strands she had caught back with a blue band which matched her dress. "I don't see why you're fussing," he said briefly, "but we can certainly take the time. Another four hours driving will get us to Lyon without any trouble." He swallowed some coffee before observing to the front page of his newspaper, "You should see a doctor instead of a hairdresser. I noticed you're still limping."

"Nope. I'm practically as good as new."

"You are an obstinate creature," he said with detachment.

"Determined is the polite word." While reaching for more marmalade, she managed a closer look at him and discovered some lines around his eyes that weren't there the day before. "You're a little on the frazzled side yourself. What's the matter? Wasn't the couch comfortable?"

He folded his newspaper to another page. "It was fine, thanks," he said briefly in the tone of a man who wants to close the subject.

"I told you we should have changed places," she persisted. "Anybody could see that davenport was a foot too short for you."

"The davenport was fine." This time there was no hiding his irritation. "Is there any more so-called coffee in the pot?"

She waggled it experimentally and nodded. "Plenty." Taking his cup and refilling it, she asked, "Are you mad at the coffee too?"

"I'm *not* mad," he started in heatedly and then broke off, looking sheepish. "Sorry, I'm not at my best at this time of day. Usually I don't have to put it to a test."

Which meant, Carolyn decided, that his relationship with the beauteous Gina wasn't as torrid as she had believed. Either that or the Italian thoughtfully made herself scarce at breakfast time. She looked over at Michael again. It could be a frank appraisal this time because he was again engrossed in his paper. His absorption was scarcely flattering, she concluded, even though her hair did need fixing.

"Then it's all right if we take the morning off. . . ." she reaffirmed.

"Ummm." He didn't look up.

Her eyes narrowed and she continued in a bright voice. "Or perhaps I should climb a tall building . . ."

"Uh-huh."

"And throw myself off the top story."

"Whatever you say," he muttered absently into the sports page. "My God! Who seeded that Hungarian twelfth in the Wimbledon ratings? He hasn't any net game at all."

There was a violent scrape of the chair opposite him and he looked up to see Carolyn disappearing into the bedroom, slamming the door behind her.

For a moment, he stared at the closed door and then his lips twisted in a grimace that was hard to interpret.

There were no further altercations for the rest of the morning. Carolyn went to the hairdressers and emerged after an hour and a half with a new hair style which made her feel happier about her chances with the masculine sex in general and possibly one in particular. She also decided to change her behavior to go along with the new hairdo. It couldn't hurt to present a softer, more feminine appearance in every way.

When she met Mike in the pedestrian mall by the hotel at noon she waited anxiously for his reaction. It wasn't long coming.

He got up from a bench where he had been lazing in the pale sunshine and surveyed her approvingly. "Very nice. I like that fringe effect or whatever it is."

She flushed under his intent gaze. "Thanks. You found my note, I see."

He nodded. "The desk clerk handed it over when I got back from putting the bags in the car." His mouth curved upward. "Have you any more written instructions or are we back to speaking to each other?"

"We didn't ever officially stop speaking. Breakfast could be called a communications gap." He remained tactfully silent and she went on, "Since we have a while before the afternoon newspapers hit the streets with their sports pages . . ."

"Let's make the most of it." He took her elbow and steered her purposefully back toward the hotel. "I could do with some lunch."

"There's a sandwich shop up this street."

He kept walking in the opposite direction. "No deal. They cut the sandwich bread so thin over here that it takes four to fill a man up."

"I noticed that yesterday during our picnic. I thought I was going to lose my second half."

"Teaches you not to dawdle over your food." He was forced to stop as she lingered in front of an antique shop window. "Now what?"

Caro pointed to a crudely carved wooden spoon resting on a pile of mismatched kitchen cutlery. "I wonder what that is?" Then hastily, "And don't say, 'a spoon, obviously.' "

"Didn't even think of it," he said with a virtuous expression. When she pressed her forehead against the window, he added, "We'll never find out if we don't go in and ask . . . but no dallying."

"Not much," she temporized, ducking under his arm as a brass bell on the shop door heralded their arrival.

A stooped, gray-haired man wearing thick glasses emerged from a curtained back room. "Good day," he said. "Could I help you?"

Carolyn pointed toward the display. "That wooden spoon in the window . . ." she moved over by it. "Could I see it, please?"

"Of course." Slowly he made his way to the cluttered window and took it from the pile of cutlery for her inspection. "This will be something new for you if you're Canadians or . . ."

"Americans," Mike supplied as he peered at the wooden object in Carolyn's hand. The spoon was about nine inches long with a thin carved handle at least two inches wide.

"I've never seen anything quite like it," she confessed. "Does it have a special significance?"

The old man nodded enthusiastically. "Indeed yes! Here in Wales we call them Sweetheart Spoons and the originals are hard to find these days." Then he shrugged apologetically, "Of course, there isn't any intrinsic value to speak of but there is a charming history."

"A 'Sweetheart Spoon,'" mused Carolyn, turning it over carefully in her fingers. "Then the carved symbols have a meaning?"

"Certainly, miss . . . and this spoon has most of the traditional ones." A wrinkled finger came over the counter top to trace them. "There's a chain . . . that's for loyalty—the shackle stands for life. The twisting represents two lives together and, of course, the heart up at the top of the spoon means love. Years ago, each Welsh country lad whittled one of these for his sweetheart. If she accepted it, it would be hung in her house to warn off any other suitors." The network of lines on the old man's face deepened as he smiled benevolently. "These spoons were where the word 'spooning' originally came from," he added.

"It's a lovely story." Carolyn caressed the smooth worn wood with her thumb. "And this is far too nice to be left in a shop window."

The shop owner agreed. "A very appropriate gift for a man to his chosen one." He looked toward Mike expectantly.

Caro spoke up first. "Why don't you buy this for Gina? I'm sure she'd be thrilled."

Mike backed away slightly. "According to the legend, I'm supposed to whittle one."

The shop owner cannily observed the turn of events. "I think," he put in obligingly, "that the legend would work in the same way if a man bought an old one for his sweetheart."

"Of course it would." Carolyn stroked the carved spoon once more and then handed it to Mike. "You must buy it for her. Any woman would love a Sweetheart Spoon. . . ."

"Why don't you keep it. . . . I'd like you to have it. It can be a souvenir of Swansea."

She put her hands behind her back and shook her head stubbornly. "That would spoil the magic. You heard what the man said—a Sweetheart Spoon has to be given with love." Her glance moved along the counter. "If you really want to buy me something, that ceramic tile over there would be nice for the top of my bookshelf. At least I think it would . . . provided the words on it don't say something like 'Souvenir of the Cardiff

Livestock Exposition.' " She looked inquiringly at the clerk. "What does 'Deuwch pan fynnoch, croeso pan ddeloch' mean?"

He shook his head in gentle amusement over her stumbled pronunciation. "It says, 'Come when you will, and welcome when you come.' "

"Oh, that's charming," she said in some relief. "I'd love to have it for my living room." She added firmly to Mike, "But you must buy the Sweetheart Spoon for Gina as well."

He smiled and made a gesture of surrender to the shop owner. "You heard the lady. I'll take both of them."

"Would you make separate parcels, please?" Carolyn gave a last tiny pat to the spoon which Mike put down on the counter.

"Of course, miss." The old gentleman rooted about until he found two wrinkled pieces of paper and succeeded in achieving two lumpy parcels. The smaller he handed to Mike, who stuffed it in his jacket pocket, and the other was given to Carolyn, who put it carefully in her purse.

Once the proper change had been given and they were hovering by the door, the shop owner added a final caution. "I should warn you that many of our folk think there's a great deal of power in the legend of the Sweetheart Spoon." He pushed his spectacles further up on the bridge of his nose before continuing, "The man should be sure that it's given to the right woman and, of course," his voice lowered significantly, "a woman must not accept it unless she's sure as well. Otherwise ..." he put his palms to his cheeks and shook his head dismally.

There was a silence which filled the tiny shop while Mike and Carolyn absorbed those quiet words.

Then Mike nodded abruptly and said, "We'll remember, thanks," before taking Caro by the arm and ushering her out the door. Once on the sidewalk he added, "After all that mumbo-jumbo, I feel as if I'm carrying a secret weapon in my pocket. I thought the days of black magic were over in this country."

"It's not black magic. Don't you remember— love was the force which broke all the evil spells."

"Uh-huh, if you say so. Let's get back to the hotel," he said carelessly but he patted his pocket to make sure the package was still there.

They strolled down the busy sidewalk jammed with noontime shoppers. At their side, the Swansea shops were a curious blend of modern and traditional. Tiny restaurant bars featuring signs of "Coffees" and "Teas" were full of patrons who either perched on stools or stood elbow to elbow, the air thick with their conversation and laughter. A delivery man who was whistling cheerily brushed by Carolyn and she stared after him.

"These people should be in the cast of a musical comedy," she told Mike.

"Maybe they're just less inhibited than we are.

I read somewhere that when three Englishmen get together they form a club but three Welshmen form a choir."

"Well, it's a nice change anyway."

He nodded. "And after yesterday, you deserve . . ." His words broke off as she clutched his arm. "What is it?"

"That van!" She pointed down the street. "It looked like the one that knocked me down. Oh darn! It's gone around the corner. Now we'll never know."

He gave her shoulder a commiserating squeeze. "There's no use getting your hopes up. Probably the one you saw at Chepstow is at the other end of the country by now."

"Or back in London at the home office."

His mouth took on grim lines. "No, not at the home office."

"What do you mean?"

"I was going to tell you during lunch." He moved aside to let a woman wheel a monumental British pram past them. "You could put triplets in one of those things," he muttered.

"I'll remember that if the occasion ever arises," she said with irony. "Now—go on about the truck."

"There's not much to tell. I called the London office of Wellington Foods while you were having your hair done. They don't have any vans delivering in Wales. Their trucks only work in the metropolitan areas of London and Edinburgh. Incidentally, they're all painted a bright green."

"So there goes all the evidence," Carolyn said, stopping outside the hotel entrance. "I guess it's a good thing I wasn't killed."

"I guess so," he replied just as solemnly. "Come on . . . cheer up. We can't have the Welsh thinking that all Americans go around with long faces." He watched her smile faintly. "That's better. You'll feel happier after lunch. They have a complete list of sandwiches on the menu . . ." He backed away from her threatening hand. "I thought that would get a rise out of you. All right, I'll buy you a steak and kidney pie instead."

"That's big of you."

He held the door open for her. "It's self-preservation too. I imagine this castle of yours is long on ghosts and short on food."

"I honestly don't know," she admitted. "There's a caretaker on the premises to let me in. Surely he'll provide food as well."

He shook his head pityingly. "Lord! You're still wet behind the ears! We'll allow an extra fifteen minutes on our schedule this afternoon."

"What for?"

"A trip to the nearest grocery store," he said firmly. "If we're going to storm the castle, let's be fully prepared."

She grinned over her shoulder at him. "A modern Don Quixote with a lance of French bread."

"Make it English seed cake," he corrected. Intercepting her puzzled look, he explained, "That stuff's heavy enough to kill anybody."

She paused in the archway of the dining room. "One thing I *do* know ... after listening to your jokes for two days, even the ghosts of Lyonsgate Castle will sound good."

He merely caught the headwaiter's eye and murmured, "We'll see, Miss Drummond, we'll see."

Her morale was in good shape after a satisfying and well-served luncheon. They drove cheerfully out of the busy port town with its cracking towers and chemical plants extending for miles in the industrial areas. The famous Swansea precipitation stacks loomed high in a cloudless sky.

Soon their narrow two-lane road took them through a more rugged countryside and they drove on through picturesque Pembroke toward the coast. The neat clusters of gray stone houses thinned and were gradually replaced with rolling grassy pastures tenanted by fat sheep or well-cared-for cattle.

The hours passed pleasantly and Carolyn was still in an uncaring haze brought on by the leisurely drive and the bucolic scenery, when the sudden appearance of Lyonsgate's stark silhouette on a hillside at dusk sent a shiver of fear coursing through her.

The castle was constructed on sheer rock overlooking the turbulent waters of the Bay of Martyrs. At one end, the main tower loomed up in the shape of an ancient halberd while around its gray stone base, grass grew in patches and tufts like hair edging a bald pate. The extensive castle grounds were thickly covered with trees, and uncut meadows extended from either side of the building.

It looked, Carolyn decided, like an abandoned city park.

"Nothing that a dozen gardeners couldn't put right in six months," Mike said, proving that he was on her wave length again. "I hope your employer has plenty of money."

"He has."

He nodded grimly. "He'll need it. I think it would be cheaper if he tried to buy Lichtenstein or Luxembourg."

"I didn't realize Lyonsgate would be so big."

Mike let the car slow perceptibly as he turned onto a gravel track marked only with a small wooden sign that said "Castle."

"I've never thought about it before," he admitted, "but I don't suppose honest-to-God castles come in very small sizes. Compared to Windsor, this is certainly an afterthought, but it's still big enough to house a Moose convention without crowding."

Carolyn was gazing up at the pointed lancet windows dotting the main tower. "How do they ever clean that glass?"

He shook his head silently and waved toward a

wing protruding from the central structure. "Take a look at that battlement with the two bartizans."

She peered obediently through the windshield. "I know what a battlement is ... but what's a bartizan?"

"That round overhang at the end. They used them for defense. The notches on the top of it are crenels...." He stared through the dusk. "My lord, those must be original arrow slits."

Carolyn was rummaging in her bag and came out with a long typed paper. "They are," she said consulting it. She read on: "The castle boasts its own chapel wing, remnants of an old dungeon used before Cromwell's time, and ..."

"And a stone fence with an iron gate," Mike said, stopping the car abruptly. "This is it."

"With stone lions on either side of it," murmured Caro. "Just like the name."

"Are you sure you were expected?"

She nodded. "An estate office in London set up the appointment. There's supposed to be a caretaker somewhere."

"A gatekeeper would be more helpful," Mike groused. "I'll look around, but we may have to drive back to the last wide spot in the road and hope there's a telephone up in that pile of rocks."

Carolyn wished she could shrug off the feeling of foreboding that the castle gave her. "Did the nobles believe in things like telephones? I thought you sent out a knight on a quest or a carrier pigeon with a message."

"Probably it was a serving wench with a folded note tucked in a strategic place," he agreed with a mild leer.

She watched him get out of the car. "Well, if you run into any comely serving wenches on this trip, ask if they have a key tucked in a strategic place. It's cold around here."

There was the flash of his grin before he marched up to the heavy wrought-iron gates. He peered cautiously through them and Carolyn let out a soft sigh. Thank heavens, she hadn't been forced to come to this dismal place alone. The damp night air seemed to penetrate the car in salty waves. Grimly, she turned up her jacket collar and huddled down in the seat.

"I'll be damned!" Mike's epithet startled her out of her reverie.

"What did you find?" she called.

The creak of protesting iron answered her and she saw him push open the heavy gate with his shoulder.

"You mean it was open all along?" she persisted.

"Evidently." He shouted back without turning around as he made short work of the second gate by using a good-sized rock to wedge it open.

She watched him stride back to the car, as he wiped his hands on a handkerchief. "Didn't the lock work?" she asked when he settled beside her, bringing a rush of cold air as well.

"It hasn't worked in a couple of centuries. It's a good thing too. Those gates are so high, you'd have to have sat on my shoulders even if we'd had a key." He started the car and proceeded carefully up the drive. "Evidently they didn't want the neighbors to drop in."

Carolyn inspected the elaborate gate as they went past. "That caused all the trouble."

"What did?"

"The neighbors dropping in around here. I was reading about it. They did it for hundreds of years—bringing their crossbows and boiling oil along for hostess gifts. When Cromwell's troops came, they laid siege to the castle and the ownership changed hands."

"Hardly friendly of them," Mike agreed.

"But six months later, the invaders were thrown out and things went back to the status quo." She saw his shoulders heave with silent laughter. "What's the matter?"

"Nothing." The word came out with difficulty. "Except that I'd like to see a history professor's face if he heard your abbreviated version of the Siege of the Roundheads."

"Sorry. It *was* slightly condensed."

"Don't apologize to me—I liked it. You'd better curb your explanations if the castle's owner is around, though."

"He's not apt to be. The London firm said that

70

he was stationed somewhere in the Far East with the British Foreign Service. I can just see him—drooping walrus mustache and stiff upper lip. Do you suppose he talks about the good old days in 'Injah'?"

"Most of those types went out with Neville Chamberlain. Haven't you seen the mod generation in Piccadilly Circus lately?"

She made a face. "Heavens yes! All bells and beads. The girls' skirts are either micro or maxi ... nothing in between." She absently smoothed a wrinkle from her jacket before asking, "I wonder if we should have closed that front gate?"

"Not when I'm doing a round trip. There's no point in making extra work."

"But surely you'll stay for dinner ..." She broke off, suddenly aware that she was scarcely in a position to invite guests for dinner since it wasn't her castle.

"Exactly." He was reading her mind again as he negotiated a gentle curve on the drive. "Don't worry about me."

"You're not going to drive back to Swansea tonight? It's almost dark now."

"Is that bad?" he asked with some amusement.

"No—but it *is* a long way." She peered out of the car window as they neared the castle. "Obviously there's an extra guest room somewhere in there."

"Now look," he said firmly, "this is your castle and I refuse to be included in the package deal.

I'll make sure that you're squared away for the night and then I'll drive back to the nearest village. The pub can probably handle an overnight guest."

Carolyn thought that he needn't appear so happy to get rid of her. Aloud, she said stiffly, "Whatever you like," but as he stopped in front of the massive entrance she added, "I think you're being unnecessarily stubborn . . . as usual."

He merely raised an eyebrow for an answer as he removed the key from the ignition. "Let's find the caretaker, shall we? If we're at the wrong door, it'll take another fifteen minutes to find our way to the back."

"All right." She crawled out of the car and hovered uneasily on the lowest stone step. "It's awfully quiet, isn't it?"

"No one could say that a castle is cozy." He came around the car and joined her, peering at the unkempt shrubbery which bordered the steps. Someone had made an attempt to cut the grass in front of the entrance but the ragged edges revealed more enthusiasm than talent. The boxwood hedge surrounding the large fountain in the center of the lawn was already beginning to look like a hedgerow rather than a trimmed border.

"What a pity," Mike said, surveying it. "Somebody originally tried some topiary on that—a lot of work to go to seed."

Carolyn followed his glance. "It's just the sort

72

of thing that old Henry would love despite the neglect. He'd like that stone lion in the fountain too and if I know my employer, he'll uncover a genealogy chart to prove he's a direct descendant from all this."

"Throwing in Richard the Lion-Hearted for good measure, I suppose."

"Good heavens, did he sleep here too?"

"I don't think so. He liked the warm winters in Cyprus."

"*Now* who's fiddling with history?"

"Enough of the chitter-chatter." He put a firm hand on her arm. "Come on, let's storm the castle walls and get you inside the place. It's cold out here."

They paused in front of the elaborately carved entrance door.

"How do we get in?" she whispered. "There isn't a knocker or a bell."

"I guess we pull that chain. It either rings a bell somewhere or tips a bucket of boiling oil down from the parapet." He clamped onto her wrist as she took a startled step backward. "Stand still, idiot! I'm just fooling." Then, reaching up, he gave a determined yank to the chain.

"Very professional. You could turn out for bell ringing." Caro was edgy and it showed in her voice. "Now what?" she added as he held up a hand.

"Shhh. I thought I heard something. I *did*...."

he announced after a second's pause. "The care-taker's on the job, after all."

The heavy door in front of them opened with a metallic screech from the hinges that would have done credit to a horror movie.

Startled, Carolyn glued herself to Mike's side like a limpet as they both stared at the tall man in the doorway.

"Good evening," he greeted them in a pleasant voice. "I'm terribly sorry about keeping you wait-ing but I wasn't expecting anyone and it takes a bit of time to get from the upper hallway. Can I help you?" He looked inquiringly at Mike.

The latter nodded. "My name is Evans ... Michael Evans. We're here regarding Miss Drum-mond's arrangements to view the property."

"Er ... yes." Carolyn stumbled over her words as she took up the cue. "The estate office in Lon-don made an appointment for me to view the castle this week." She plunged on despite the man's puzzled look. "I'm representing Mr. Henry Lyon in the United States."

"You mean there's a man named Lyon in the States who's interested in purchasing this proper-ty?" There was polite incredulity in the clipped tones.

"Of course. That's why I'm here." She was more confused than ever. "The man in London said he'd alert the caretaker. Didn't he call you?"

By her side, Mike preserved a watchful silence. Caro wondered if he was as amazed as she to find this young man in the job. He couldn't have been past his early thirties.

Her glance flickered again over the figure leaning nonchalantly against the door frame. He was slender but well over six feet. His dark hair needed cutting and fell untidily over a broad forehead which surmounted a thin, beaky nose. Prominent cheekbones emphasized his deep-set eyes and gave him an air of austere dignity which wasn't offset by his baggy sweater worn over a pair of ancient gray flannel trousers. Only his accent was impeccable, but it was the crisp speech of England, not the lilt of the Welsh countryside.

He seemed to rouse himself as her words finally penetrated. "Of course, Miss Drummond. I'm sorry for this inconvenience ... the London chap probably did tell old Reese." He saw her frown and went on, "Reese is my caretaker for Lyonsgate. Unfortunately, he's been away for a day or so."

"Then you are ... ?"

"I'm Hugh Lyon." He pulled the door wider and beamed down at her. "I own the property. Won't you come in."

"Thank you very much—we'd like to." There was no mistaking the overtone of proprietorship in Mike's voice as he nudged Carolyn through the door.

"Let me turn on some more lights so you can see properly," Hugh said, deserting them to search for switches by a mammoth oak reception table. "I'm by myself here tonight ... holding down the fort as you Americans would say." He looked over his shoulder and smiled at Carolyn. "Don't let that worry you, though. I can easily arrange overnight accommodation." He snapped the switch for the overhead chandelier. "There— that makes things brighter."

"Thank you very much," she said faintly.

"And you, Mr. Evans," Hugh turned back, "will you be staying overnight, too?"

There was the slightest pause. Mike felt, rather than saw, Carolyn's figure stiffen beside him. Was it with hope or fear?

He didn't hesitate any longer. Clearing his throat decisively, he said, "Yes thanks, I'll be here too." He was just as polite as their host, when he added, "I'd planned on staying just as long as Miss Drummond needs me."

Chapter Four

Half an hour passed before Carolyn had a chance to corner Mike and say, "In addition to your other failings, I now find that you're an unmitigated ..."

"Liar," he supplied helpfully.

"Exactly the word I had in mind."

They were alone for the moment, seated in front of a blazing fireplace in the long reception hall. There had been an attempt to furnish the area in modern comfort; a few upholstered pieces were interspersed between carved oak chests and high-backed, armless chairs. Two large tapestries covered most of the wall space and overhead, massive beams laced the whitewashed ceiling. Carolyn noted that oak was used again in the long, carved mantel above the fireplace. Two crouching lions were depicted at either end with the words *Virtute Securus* in between.

As a place for a cozy chat, she decided that the hall held all the charm of the main waiting room in New York's Penn Station.

"I thought you could use some help," Mike was saying. He winced as he tried to fit his frame into a carved chair that looked as if it should have been in a museum. From Mike's expression, he was obviously wishing the museum had found it before he did. "You couldn't be left alone here overnight with you-know-who." He jerked his head toward the hallway.

She glanced apprehensively over her shoulder. "Be quiet, or you-know-who will hear you! I can't see why it takes him so long to make a pot of coffee."

"First off, it probably takes him fifteen minutes to find the kitchen and another fifteen to struggle back. I hope you like cold coffee because that's the way it'll be." He gave up trying to find a comfortable spot on the chair and searched in his jacket for a cigarette.

"I hate cold coffee and tonight it sounds worse than usual." Carolyn shivered despite the fire in front of her. It was having singularly small effect on the draft whistling across her shoulders. "I wonder if there'll be enough hot water for a bath later on?"

"Probably," he said comfortingly as he extracted a cigarette and lighted it. "If not, there's bound to be an antique warming pan somewhere in the castle and we can fill it with hot coals from the fireplace."

"I'll settle for a hot water bottle, thanks. My *own* hot water bottle."

He stared at her as if she were a rare species. "What do you know.... I didn't think women still carried those things."

Her chin came up. "Evidently you only consort with the hot-blooded Italian types but for the rest of us ..."

"The cold-blooded ones, you mean...." he baited.

"Exactly ... er, certainly not!" She glared at him. "Oh, you're impossible!" Approaching footsteps made her discontinue the discussion, but she folded her arms defiantly across her breast, partly in anger and partly trying to add some warmth to her shivering frame.

Hugh Lyon came into view carrying a round silver tray topped with a chipped earthenware coffeepot and three cups and saucers which looked priceless even at twenty feet away.

"I'm frightfully sorry to have taken so long," he apologized. "Mrs. Reese, the caretaker's wife, has a strange storage system in the kitchen and I don't get there often enough to fathom it." He put the tray on a nearby table and sorted out the china. "Probably this coffee has gotten a little cold—I hope you don't mind."

"Not at all," Caro murmured politely, and avoided glancing at Mike.

"We're out of milk or cream until tomorrow but you Americans take it black, don't you?"

"That's right," Mike answered cheerfully and stared with amusement at the other American, who, he remembered, preferred both cream and sugar.

Hugh took his own cup and sank onto the couch with every evidence of enjoyment. "Frankly, I'm so delighted to be back in this part of the world where you don't have to purify the water before you can make the coffee that anything is all right."

Carolyn belatedly remembered her manners. "This tastes very good," she said carefully. "I understand you've been stationed in the Far East."

The other nodded and accepted one of Mike's cigarettes. "Burma," he confirmed, leaning forward for a light. "Four years—four long years."

"I thought diplomatic life was one long glamorous whirl," she commented.

He flashed her a confidential grin. "That's what they tell the junior clerks when they're recruiting. Just between us, it gets jolly boring. Four years of diplomatic receptions with the same three topics discussed at every one."

"What *do* people discuss at diplomatic receptions?" Carolyn asked, her coffee forgotten.

"First, they come up and say 'How long you been in Rangoon'? Next, they said 'How many children you got?' Finally we whizzed into that Dale Carnegie favorite of 'Hot, isn't it.' " Hugh shuddered. "Imagine—four years of that!"

Both Carolyn and Mike burst into laughter.

"Foreign Service intrigues in the movies will never be the same again," she admitted. "You've shattered our illusions."

"I know," Hugh said. "I shouldn't have admitted it, but it was to help you understand how splendid it is for me to be home again. Even if this cold, weak British coffee," he said with an amused look, "probably offends your righteous American tastes."

"We bow to your diplomacy," Mike said, raising his cup in salute while Carolyn blushed. "I understand why the British Foreign Service usually makes us look like country cousins."

"Now we've settled that so splendidly, you must be wondering where you're going to sleep." Hugh pushed upward, unfolding his length easily. "Actually you'll find the rest of the night worse than the coffee. The rooms are prepared, but the beds haven't been aired." He turned to ask Carolyn, "Is that a problem where you live?"

She shook her head. "Not in my one-bedroom apartment."

"But you have central heating?" He made it sound like the original sin.

"They come that way," she said meekly, "but I'm sure we'll be very comfortable here." This was an afterthought as they moved in a body toward the long curving stair and even chillier air.

Once she saw the room assigned to her, she wasn't as positive.

For the first time she understood why Guinevere had left King Arthur in Cardiff Castle to flee with Sir Lancelot to France. Probably the wily Frenchman had dangled a warm bedroom as incentive and Guinevere, frozen stiff after a winter in Wales, leaped to follow him.

Hugh was hovering anxiously in the doorway as she glanced up. "This is lovely," she said truthfully, "but I'm overwhelmed. I've never slept in a room this big." Her gesture encompassed the whitewashed chamber which would have easily accommodated seven ladies from a Turkish harem.

In the middle of one wall stood a magnificent canopied bed, its maroon hangings and coverings still elegant despite the imprint of time. Two immense armoires were arranged on either side and Caro swallowed a laugh as she looked at them. The contents of her suitcases could easily be fitted into the end of one.

Opposite, there was a gaping fireplace where Hugh had evidently kindled a blaze while on his trip to make coffee. The flames had tried hard but the warmth barely made itself felt in the chilly room.

"I'm not used to all this," Carolyn said feebly

and only the sudden, amused gleam in Michael's eyes revealed that he understood her meaning.

Hugh accepted it as the conventional remark. "At least we have adequate plumbing. My grandfather installed some extra bathrooms so you don't have to wander down the cold halls the way they used to."

Chalk up another talking point for Sir Lancelot, Carolyn thought.

"You must have missed all this when you were stationed in Burma," Mike said pleasantly.

Hugh shook his head. "It was only through a fluke that I inherited a few years ago." A tinge of bitterness crept into his tone. "If I'm not exactly enthusiastic about the ancestral acres, it's because my mother took me back to live with her family in France when I was rather small. My memories of this spot aren't all fond ones. That's one reason I've put the castle up for sale." He turned to Mike, who was lounging against the door. "If you know anything about British death duties, you can figure out the other reasons."

"I've heard they're pretty steep."

"That's an understatement. I hope your Mr. Lyon in America decides he needs a castle."

"He's not my Mr. Lyon," Mike pointed out. "I'm just along for the ride. Miss Drummond is your prospect."

"Then I'll use my energy convincing her." Hugh's attention was back on Carolyn, his smile indicating it wasn't any hardship.

"If I could fill my hot water bottle, it would be a start," she replied meekly. The prospect of damp sheets in that mammoth bed made her shudder.

"Of course. Would you like more coffee as a nightcap?"

"No thanks ... just the hot water bottle. If you'll wait a minute, I'll find it for you." She opened her overnight bag, which Mike had deposited on a low chest and rummaged for her prized possession.

"It's a good thing you brought one," Hugh admitted. "I'm not sure where the Reeses store ours."

"Have they been with you long?" Mike asked idly. "Your caretakers, I mean," he added, grinning.

Hugh was tending the fire. "Years and years. The few pleasant memories I have of this place concern old Reese. His wife speaks only Welsh, you know, so that rather limits our communication, but the old chap couldn't be more obliging. Fortunately, they're better-than-average cooks, so we'll manage nicely." He stood up and dusted his hands. "Perhaps you'd like a snack of something now before bed?"

Mike, whose stomach was protesting the lack of dinner, looked brighter.

Carolyn brushed the suggestion aside. "Don't worry about food. We've been eating too much ever since we got to Wales."

"Well, if you're sure . . ." their host agreed.

Mike directed a look at Carolyn which would have squelched a less-determined woman, but she returned it defiantly.

"I think we should go to bed," she said without thinking.

Mike was caught off-guard but rallied quickly and decided to have some fun. "Whatever you say, darling." He ignored her surprised look and came over to drape a possessive arm around her shoulders. "Let me know if you need me later tonight, won't you?"

It was time for Hugh to turn and stare. Obviously he was reassessing the relationship between his guests and Carolyn didn't care for his conclusion.

She shrugged hastily out of that affectionate clasp and shoved her hot water bottle into Mike's unwilling hand. "You can help Hugh fill this," she said sweetly.

He dangled the limp rubber bag in front of him like a very dead fish. "Thanks a lot," he managed finally. "Sure you'll be okay in here?"

"I'll be fine."

"There's no need to worry," Hugh put in. "My room is at the end of the corridor. . . ."

"And mine?" Mike asked pointedly.

"Two doors down and across the way. I hope you'll find it adequate."

In traveler's terms, those words generally meant that the mattress sagged and the fireplace chimney smoked, Mike had found. He began to understand why Cromwell's forces had quit the castle after only six months.

"The hot water bottle ..." Carolyn suggested again hopefully. She flexed her cold fingers and wondered if frostbite settled in overnight.

"The hot water bottle, of course!" Hugh took up his cue. "And I'll bring it back personally after I've settled Mr. Evans in his quarters."

"Thanks so much." She tried to sound enthusiastic. "This will be a wonderful experience ... staying in a real castle, I mean. I'll probably have insomnia just from the excitement."

Her prophetic declaration came back to haunt her later that night.

When she looked at her watch for the umpteenth time and found it was only eleven forty-five, she made a firm resolve never to say unkind things about modern hotels ever again.

The fire had long since collapsed into a feeble bed of coals which were taking on a gray cast even as she watched. The strong draft was whistling the last warm air up the chimney to proclaim its official demise.

Carolyn sighed and looked away. She was still fully dressed, but she had changed into an ankle-length wool lounging skirt topped by the thickest sweater she owned. The thought of shedding her outfit for a pair of nylon pajamas and crawling into that monster of a bed was still too awful to consider.

The cold sheets weren't the only things that had her heart beating faster than usual. Half an hour before, a series of muffled noises had roused her from her paperback novel. She had looked up briefly, decided that all castles creaked in cold weather like ordinary houses, and plunged back into Chapter Four.

Twenty minutes later, the next disturbance brought her head up sharply. Evidently termites who lived in castles, she decided with a frown, grew bigger than the ones in apartment houses. That time she put the book down and prowled uneasily around the room.

Surely Hugh Lyon wasn't spending the night crawling behind her bedroom walls trying to frighten off a perfectly good real estate prospect! She clenched her teeth together to keep them from chattering. If only Liz were here! Even intruders from the spirit world wouldn't daunt old Henry's personal secretary. By now, she'd be out on the landing telling the ghosts to pack up and come back at a decent hour.

Carolyn walked purposefully over to the nearest wall and put her ear to it. Nothing. At least nothing now, she amended, and wandered over to the window to stare out at the overcast night.

If she opened the glass, she would hear the sea, Hugh had said. Her hand went out to the latch, then she took another look at the murky darkness and drew it back. It was obviously a long way down to bedrock and it didn't help her morale to stand there thinking about it.

Irritably she turned and paced across the room. If those miserable noises would only persist, she could try to identify the sounds or at least determine their source. Unfortunately, their duration was seldom more than a half-minute at a time and the effect so muffled it was difficult to pinpoint.

At first she had thought of calling either Michael or Hugh to her aid but she soon decided that she would appear to be a raving maniac or a neurotic female who imagined bumps in the night. Undoubtedly the noises would become nonexistent at the crucial time as well. Welsh haunts performed exactly like squeaks in car innards when you summoned a mechanic—they disappeared. The only thing for her to do was sit in solitary grandeur and watch the clock hands go around. Or was it?

She could at least take the Swansea tile from her purse and pack it away in her suitcase. Happy to have found a diversion, she carefully lifted it out onto her lap so that she could admire it again. "Come when you will and welcome when you come"—her finger slowly traced the ornate letters. It was really a charming remembrance. Then, unbidden, her thoughts went back to the wooden Sweetheart Spoon with its carved handle telling a love story.

"I hope to heaven his precious Gina appreciates it," she muttered to herself.

Her face looked wan and unhappy when she noted her reflection in the wavy old mirror on the opposite wall. What an idiot she was—moping over silly memories! She straightened determinedly and went over to her suitcase to tuck the tile under a pile of lingerie. At least she could make sure her keepsake got home in good condition.

It was then that the noise came again; so distinct this time that Carolyn froze in terror. There was definitely a moan of pain but it was muffled abruptly in the odd thumpings she had heard before.

She clutched her throat in indecision and then tiptoed across the room to listen at the wall. Already the thudding was getting fainter—becoming a hollow sound that reverberated like an echo. A few seconds more and it was gone again.

"Damn!" The word came out in a soft wail and she chewed on a knuckle in sheer frustration. To think of staying in her room and meekly waiting for the next session was completely unnerving. Whoever had uttered that cry of pain needed help! "And he isn't the only one," she decided, swallowing a sob. "I do too."

It was a tremendous relief to pull her quilted jacket over her shoulders and step out into the hall, leaving the door partially ajar to provide some light. Now ... which was Mike's room? What had Hugh said ... across the way and one ... no ... two doors down. She paused in front of

89

a heavily carved door and raised her hand to knock.

If he laughs, I'll kill him, she thought fiercely as she tapped faintly on the panel.

There was no response.

She knocked again, this time with more determination.

The door was pulled abruptly open and she almost continued her tattoo on Mike's broad chest.

His greeting was scarcely ecstatic. He frowned and stood his ground, growling, "What the devil are you doing here?"

"Well, I'm *not* selling brushes in the hall," she hissed indignantly. "For heaven's sake, let me in."

He passed a hand wearily over his face before moving aside so she could sweep past. "Okay—now you're in," he said. "What gives?" He closed the door quietly and leaned against it.

She clasped her hands in front of her from sheer nervousness as she walked over to the fireplace. Subconsciously she noted that their living quarters had at least two things in common; there was another huge, moldy-looking bed and another room temperature near the freezing mark.

"Your fire has gone out, too," she murmured.

He made a grimace of amusement at that and strolled over to perch on the end of the bed. "If you're selling kindling, I'll take all you've got. So what else is new?"

Some time during the evening, he'd changed into a wool shirt and heavy trousers and added a thick sweater. From his wide-awake look and the undisturbed condition of the bed, Carolyn gathered that he wasn't expecting an early night either.

Mike's eyes narrowed as he watched her prowl the room. "You didn't come here to talk about rubbing sticks together...."

"No, but it would be a wonderful idea." She eyed his dying fire with resignation. Now that it was time to explain her reason for the intrusion, the words came hard. Her glance fell on an immense brown bearskin rug by the hearth and she went down on her knees to stare at the yellowed fangs bared in perpetual snarl. "There isn't anything like this in my room. Where do you suppose they got it?"

"Maybe Mrs. Cromwell bought it at a Christmas bazaar. How the hell do I know?"

"You needn't growl at me," she flared back. "If you'll remember, you were being mighty free with your invitations earlier in the evening. I shudder to think what kind of an impression you gave Hugh."

"This is a damned silly time to pick a fight." He made a production out of looking at his watch. "Look, Carolyn," he said, trying to adopt a reasonable tone, "it's late. Much too late for you to be wandering around strange rooms ... unless you have a reason for it." He ignored the flush that was creeping along her cheekbones and added sternly, "A *good* reason."

She collapsed on the thick animal rug and ran a finger down Poppa Bear's moth-eaten nose. "I heard noises. . . ." Her gaze was kept fixed on two unlikely glass eyes, but she heard a disgusted snort from the end of the bed. "Lots of noises," she burst out, looking up. "The last time somebody groaned too."

Michael stood up and held out his hand. "Come on. I'll take you back and prove you're imagining things."

"Oh no, you don't!" She shook her head with finality. "*You* go ahead. I'm staying here. I've been frozen stiff for hours—in more ways than one. If there was a train in the neighborhood, I'd be halfway to London by now. Old Henry can check out his own haunts from now on."

"You're being silly. It's probably because you're tired. . . ."

"I hope so. Frankly, I was about to crawl up the wall. Why didn't Hugh say something about the nightly stage show?"

"He's only been back a few days. Maybe he hasn't heard it."

"You can spare me that dubious look," she told him irritably. "I certainly don't make a habit of hearing groans in the wall."

He paused halfway to the door. "You're sure it was a groan?"

She started to nod and then shook her head

slowly. "Not really," she admitted. "It sounded like someone in pain but it stopped so suddenly that it was hard to tell. When I got over to the wall . . . everything was finished."

"How often did you hear these noises?"

"Three times—about twenty minutes apart." She checked her watch. "If they stay on schedule, the curtain should go up in about five minutes."

"Okay. I'll go hang around and see what happens."

"Mike!" Her call brought him back from the hallway. "Are you going to tell Hugh?"

"Not right now." Noting her relieved expression, he went on to explain, "I'm still not convinced myself. If you start hearing noises in here, turn the bear loose on them." He closed the door firmly behind him before she could find an answer.

Left alone, Carolyn stirred uneasily. Just then, she wasn't sure whether she wanted Mike to hear those noises or not. It would be reassuring to have her fears confirmed; on the other hand, it would be equally reassuring to be told that the old castle walls were merely responding to atmospheric changes. But since when, asked her conscience, did atmospheric changes cause beams to groan in the night?

She sighed deeply and wished Mike were back. Then her lips curved upward as she patted the worn bearskin rug. "You're not much company, friend," she told it. The beady eyes stared malevolently back as the last flicker of firelight gleamed in them.

Idly she ran her fingers down the yellowed fangs and found herself hoping that Michael wasn't disposed to walk in his sleep.

"A person would limp for weeks if he stumbled into your bicuspids," she murmured respectfully.

Poppa Bear fortunately made no response and her smile became more enthusiastic. She could never admit to Mike that she was hearing voices here as well!

She stood up and went over to the hall door to check. There was nothing. Not even the faint whistle of the wind from the sea could be heard on this side of the corridor.

She moved back into the center of the room and finally detoured to sit on the edge of the big bed. Now that she had told Michael of her fears, her tenseness was starting to melt away. She yawned once—and then once again. Finally she decided that it wouldn't hurt to see if the pillows were possible.

Once the faded velvet spread was turned back, the long pillows in their snowy linen bolsters were a pleasant surprise. Evidently Mrs. Reese had kept them properly "aired."

Carolyn pushed the spread back still further and shrugged off her loafers before putting her stockinged feet up on the comforter. She might as well rest while Mike was waiting in her room. Her eyelids drooped as she leaned down to pull the spread back over her legs. Somehow it seemed warmer up on the bed. Probably, she decided hazily, because it was a feather mattress. She shifted her shoulders comfortably—it was like sinking into a lovely warm hole.

I should have tried it before, she thought, and spared a moment of remorse for Michael who hadn't had time to try it at all.

Probably he had been pacing the floor wishing that his beautiful Gina wasn't so far away. Her eyelids fluttered wide open on that idea and she raised her head to rearrange her pillow. She vigorously pounded a depression in the feathers and resolved to put further thoughts of the Italian girl to the back of her mind. After that, all she had to do was think of someone else.

Flopping back down on the pillow, she went quickly through a list of possibles and happily settled on Hugh Lyon's profile.

It was nice to arouse a gleam in any man's eyes—especially one as presentable as the British diplomat. After being exposed to Mike's casual treatment for the past two days, the attention was doubly welcome.

She flounced again on the mattress remembering Hugh's abrupt leave-taking after he had delivered the filled hot water bottle. His "good night" would certainly have been more protracted if Mike hadn't hovered so protectively in the background all the while.

There was no getting around it, she decided.

Mike would have to be told that she was quite capable of looking after herself. Once he understood that, things would be different. It was on that thought and with her lips curved in anticipation that Carolyn fell soundly asleep.

She had no idea what time it was when she felt Mike's hand shaking her shoulder.

"Carolyn—wake up! You have to get out of here," he whispered forcefully.

Her eyelids fluttered up halfway. "Why? Did you find the ghosts?" The words were slurred with sleep.

"I didn't find anything except a mouse in the back of one of those damned cupboards."

"Maybe he stomped around behind the walls." She turned her back to him. "I'm awfully sleepy. Why don't you go 'way?"

The hand descended on her shoulder again. "*You* go away. This is *my* bed, remember?"

"I won't go back in that room tonight and you'd better not, either. Imagine what Hugh would think if he found you there in the morning." The lack of logic in her reasoning obviously escaped her.

Mike frowned down at her recumbent body. "Then what the hell do you expect me to do?"

He didn't hope for a coherent answer but surprisingly he got one.

"Go to bed, I s'pose." She blinked owlishly—more than half asleep. "This one's big enough for n'army. First time I've been warm tonight. It's all right, Mike...." She was painfully serious. "You're absolutely safe ... and Gina needn't know. G'night." Her hand flapped once and then pulled the spread up over her shoulders.

Mike's face was a study in contrasts as he stood staring by the bedside. So he'd be absolutely safe— and, by God, she made it sound like a compliment! As if any man wanted that award hung on him. He was torn by a desire to snatch her up and follow a choice of alternatives ... any one of which would leave her gasping.

He stood there a minute longer, leaning against the post which supported the canopy as if he too needed reinforcement to strengthen his morale. Then he turned away and carefully avoided looking in the mirror which hung on the wall nearby.

Score one for Miss Drummond! For the first time in years, Michael Evans, despite all visual evidence to the contrary, had emerged from a boudoir battle with egg on his face.

Chapter Five

It was the knocking which disturbed Carolyn the next morning. A subdued but persistent knocking which eventually penetrated the depths of her slumber and caused her to stir restlessly before opening her eyes.

Her first movement slammed her head up against something which felt like a concrete abutment for the Brooklyn Bridge. Still bleary with sleep, she pushed up on her elbows and tried to focus on what was happening. Her hazel-colored eyes stared into a pair of strange black ones just three inches away. By then completely confused, her gaze took in the two yellow fangs poised over her hand.

Her mouth had just dropped open to frame a scream which would have rocked the castle's foundations when Mike awoke on the far side of the pillow and sized up the action. Without saying a word, his hand shot out and shoved her head, face down, back into the pillow, cutting off her scream at the first gurgle.

The knocking suddenly redoubled in its efforts.

"Mr. Evans?" came the voice of an elderly man from the other side of the door. "Are you all right, sir?"

Mike noted that Carolyn's hysteria had subsided even as she was struggling to get her nose out of the pillow. Judging the glare he was getting from the corner of her eye, fear had switched abruptly to sheer temper.

"Be quiet," he hissed, "and I'll take my hand away. Don't tell everybody in Wales that you've spent the night here." The struggle, he noted with satisfaction, stopped like a shot.

"Mr. Evans?" There was a discreet rattling of the heavy bolt. "I have your morning tea, sir."

Mike erupted from the far side of the bed at the same time Carolyn was clawing her way from under the heavy spread on the near side. Their strenuous exits left the velvet bed covering bunched up on the edges but still held securely in the middle by Poppa Bear's sprawling form. With his mangy head resting in the center of the pillow bolster, he looked like a Monday morning hangover from a Halloween weekend.

"I'll be right there," Mike called for the benefit of the manservant.

"If you'll just unbolt the door, sir. . . ."

"In a minute ..." Mike was pulling off the sweater he had obviously slept in and was pawing frantically through a suitcase for his robe.

"Don't you dare let him in here!" Carolyn was almost faint with shock.

"I have to. . . ."

"But where can I go?"

Michael looked around wildly as he thrust his arms in a silk dressing gown. "How about under the bed?"

She went down on her knees only to straighten hurriedly. "There isn't room and it's all dusty!" she hissed.

"So it's dusty," he whispered back irritably. "What difference does that make? Oh, all right ... let me think." His eyes came to rest on the huge wardrobe standing by the window. "Quick!" he gestured. "In there!"

Carolyn felt like a rabbit disappearing into a burrow as she scurried in the cupboard and watched Mike close the door behind her. Through a crack, she saw him start for the hall door and then detour by the bed to hastily pull up the spread on her side and shove the pillow back into a semblance of its proper shape. Still raking his hand through his tousled hair, he finally arrived at the door and unbolted it.

The man standing on the other side looked as if he'd been graven there. He was of medium height with powerful shoulders showing under a starched white jacket. Thinning gray hair was combed back from a broad forehead, but his eyebrows were bushy and jutted over pale blue eyes. His ruddy outdoor complexion and tanned muscular hands seemed to contrast strongly with the formality of the silver tray in his grasp.

When he spoke, however, his voice was a model of drawing room decorum. "Good morning, Mr. Evans. I'm Reese. Sir Hugh thought you'd like early tea."

"Of course." Michael opened the door wider and motioned him in. "Very kind of you. Just put it down anywhere." Slowly the import of the caretaker's words penetrated. "Sir Hugh, you said?"

"Yes sir." Reese put the tea tray carefully down on a bedside table. "Sir Hugh inherited the title two years ago along with the castle, but he's just returned from abroad this past week. He had rather hoped the property might be sold before this." It was impossible to tell from Reese's expression how this affected him. "I'm sorry I wasn't here last night to assist you, but the master says he managed to find most everything. I do hope you weren't inconvenienced."

Michael shot a quick look at the wardrobe cupboard. "Not at all," he assured the other.

"You were warm enough, I trust?" Reese probed delicately.

"Of course. Why?"

The elderly man made a brief but telling gesture toward the rolled bearskin occupying the middle of the bed.

In her closet, Carolyn narrowly restrained a groan. How in the world would Mike get out of that?

Michael wondered too. "Oh, *that*."

"Yes, sir."

"Well, I wasn't going to mention it, Reese, but there was a chill in the room when the fire died down. I'd appreciate it if you wouldn't say anything to Mr. Lyon . . . er . . . Sir Hugh. Tonight will be better, I'm sure."

The other's eyelids flickered. "Certainly, sir. I'll make sure there's sufficient amount of firewood. There's also a portable heater stored in the wardrobe for extra warmth. I'll get it now . . ."

Mike moved hastily to block him. "No!" he said emphatically. And then added, "I wouldn't think of bothering you. Actually I'm very comfortable at the moment."

In the closet, Carolyn sagged against the wood in relief. If she ever got out of this unscathed, she'd never leave her room again.

Reese shrugged. "If you're sure, sir. Since you're partially dressed, I thought you might be chilled."

"Not at all," Mike was expansive with his success. "This is the best time of the day. I'm an early riser."

"I presume Miss Drummond is as well, sir?"

"Miss Drummond? What do you mean?"

"There was no answer when I knocked at her room." Reese's gaze was more alert than ever. "The bed didn't look as if it had been slept in."

Michael took refuge in affronted dignity. "Really, Reese, I'm sure there's a perfectly simple explanation. We scarcely have the right to probe into Miss Drummond's affairs ... er ... actions."

"Certainly not, Mr. Evans." Reese's tone showed dignity wasn't limited to Americans. "I wouldn't have inquired, sir, except that a Mrs. Sheppard has arrived and is asking for her. Sir Hugh is out riding, so I couldn't check with him."

"I'm sure there's a perfectly simple explanation...." It occurred to Mike that he was repeating himself so he tried again. "Miss Drummond is probably taking a walk. She was admiring your scenery when we arrived. As for the bed—well, possibly she slept in a chair by the fire." His voice gained conviction. "She said something about being chilled earlier in the evening."

The thought of a castle guest being subjected to discomfort clearly unnerved the old gentleman.

"Oh, I hope not, Mr. Evans. I'll make sure my wife airs the beds carefully today."

"Don't give it another thought." Mike moved over to the tea tray and hovered purposefully. "What time is breakfast served?"

"Generally at eight-thirty, sir ... if that's convenient." Reese moved obediently to the door.

"I'll tell Mrs. Sheppard that Miss Drummond will probably be back by then."

"I'm sure she will." There was no mistaking the conviction in Mike's words this time.

"Very well. If you require anything else, there's a pull just here...." Reese indicated a tapestry rope hanging near the door. "It rings in the kitchen."

"Fine, thanks." Mike lifted the teapot. "This should keep me well satisfied until breakfast."

Reese gave a pleased nod and allowed himself one more dubious glance at Poppa Bear's recumbent form on the bed before closing the door carefully behind him.

Mike was practically on his heels to secure the bolt on the door. He then turned to find a pale Carolyn emerging from the wardrobe.

She tottered to the bed. "Lord, the smell of mothballs was strong in there! I think I've been preserved."

Mike shoved the cup of tea toward her. "Here— take this to revive."

"Don't you want it?" She reached out hesitantly.

"I'd rather have coffee, but we can share this. There's a tooth glass in the bathroom...."

"Don't bother. You can have this cup back in a minute," she said, taking a hasty sip. "I've got to get out of here. You'd think with all these hallways and rooms that a person could move around with a little freedom."

Mike's eyebrows went up.

She continued defensively, "Well, how was I to know the caretaker ran a bed check?" She took another swallow of tea. "You didn't convince him with your story of sleeping with a bear rug, either. Why in the dickens *is* Poppa Bear in the middle of the bed?"

"It was the best I could think of at one o'clock in the morning. How was I to know you wouldn't wake up screaming when you caught sight of me on the other pillow? Even though I did stay on top of the covers," he added virtuously. "And I was not about to sleep in that damned oak box they call a chair. After all, it *is* my room."

"Such gallantry." Carolyn tried to be dignified, but it was hard with an unwashed face, uncombed hair, and wrinkled clothes. Her decision to usurp Michael's bed which had made implicit sense at midnight now loomed as outrageous behavior in the gray morning light. She couldn't honestly blame him for being angry after that grilling by Reese.

She bestowed a pat on Poppa Bear before going over toward the door. "I'm still not sure whose reputation you were trying to protect," she said, unable to resist a parting jibe.

"If you don't know," Mike growled, "then I'm sure as hell not going to explain."

It was easier to ignore that. "I'd better get dressed properly," she said, trying for a graceful exit.

"Do that little thing and try to make breakfast on time, will you?" He measured her with an assessing stare. "It would help if you could look a little more like the brisk outdoor type when you arrive."

"I'll wash my face with cold water," she informed him stiffly, "and if there's time, I can jog down the corridor and through the drawing room on the way." She unbolted the door and started to pull it open. "It's a shame I left my track shoes at home, but no one will know that I haven't been out bird-watching since six."

"In a pig's eye they won't, sweetie." The brisk, middle-aged woman who stood in the middle of the doorway greeted them brightly. "So this is what happens when I let you out of my sight—and I thought the British were slow workers." She turned Carolyn around, maneuvered her deftly back into the bedroom, and closed the door. "Old Henry's going to take a dim view of this."

"Liz . . . you have it all wrong. There's a perfectly simple explanation," Carolyn told her.

"I sincerely hope so," the older woman replied. She folded her arms over her breast and turned to Mike, who stood watching the interchange. "I'm not sure about the etiquette in this situation, but I'm Liz Sheppard."

"I gathered that," he said quietly. "My name is Evans—Mike Evans." His glance went over her in one comprehensive sweep.

Liz Sheppard's face was easy to read, with her

schoolgirl's broad brow and thick graying hair which had a tendency to flop over her forehead. The sturdy bulk of her figure was clad in an expensive but ill-chosen Donegal tweed skirt and a white wool blazer completed the tubular effect. Then a pair of clear gray eyes caused him to take another look and made folly of her nondescript costume. Her beautiful, intelligent gaze was coupled with a touch of lively humor lurking about a well-shaped mouth. Michael mentally doffed a hat in tribute; here was a woman who could charm away any opposition. It was easy to see why she was the top secretary of a powerful and wealthy man.

She was obviously amused at his silent appraisal but not yet ready for a peace treaty. "Someone should have told you, Mr. Evans, that Carolyn doesn't play in this kind of league."

Mike ignored Carolyn's gasp. "I know that, Mrs. Sheppard." He rubbed the back of his neck wearily. "Why don't you find out if there was any game scheduled before you blow the whistle?"

Her sharp eyes went round the room, taking in the bear rug still bunched on the bed and Carolyn's mussed but voluminous attire. Her lips curved upward still more as she turned back to him. "Either I owe you an apology or the seduction scene has changed since my day."

Her frank pronouncement made Carolyn seethe. "I can't win with you. . . ."

"Caro love—don't be absurd," Liz interrupted

briskly. "In that outfit of yours, any woman would remain as pure as driven snow. You look like a member of a Polar expedition." She moved over to sit in the oak chair.

Mike came to Carolyn's defense. "After you've spent a night in this place, Mrs. Sheppard, you'll understand."

"Cold?"

"Like Moose Jaw, Saskatchewan, in December."

"Since you've progressed to the state of the weather and you've finished with my morals and my clothes ..." Carolyn began ominously.

"I haven't," Liz told her, cocking her head in amusement. "Where were you when Reese delivered the tea? There certainly wasn't room for you under the bearskin in those clothes."

Mike grinned. "No pun intended but you're getting warm, Mrs. Sheppard."

"Make it Liz," the other said. "I have to catch up quickly."

"Liz, then." He bent over his suitcase to select a shirt. "Take a look at the wardrobe cupboard."

She stood up and peered inside the oak armoire. "This is big enough to hold the Marx Brothers."

"Believe it or not, they weren't in there with me this morning." Carolyn walked toward the door. "You two don't need me for this discussion—I'm still going to change my clothes."

Liz glanced over her shoulder. "I would, if I were you. Don't fuss, child. I'll be along too. Reese wouldn't understand if he found me in your Michael's room when he came to pick up the tea things."

"He is *not* my Michael."

The object of their conversation looked up from fingering a blue silk foulard, obviously more interested in his selection of a tie than the determination of his social status. "Carolyn can explain all that," he said.

"And I will . . . but not here." The younger woman led Liz firmly to the door. "Take a look out in the hallway first," she instructed her.

Liz obediently checked to see if the coast was clear. "Good idea. Better not let Reese find you returning from your morning walk via Michael's bedroom." She disappeared down the hall.

Carolyn leaned her head wearily against the door jamb. "I'm beginning to think I'll never get out of this room. So help me—I'll never set foot in a man's bedroom again."

Behind her, Michael made a muttered remark.

She turned to face him. "What did you say?"

He paused by his bathroom door. "I said you shouldn't make blanket declarations. You might feel differently some time."

"That will be the day. . . ."

"It will indeed. Believe me, it's better when you wait to be invited."

The slam of the hall door behind her could

have been heard down in the dungeons. Mike's grin widened as he went on into the bathroom and laid out his shaving gear on the basin.

Let madam think that one over for a while. She'd learn that it wasn't prudent to label any man "safe" in that careless manner of hers. He'd bet that it would take more than a long, cold night in Lyonsgate before she invaded his room again.

The truth of his remark suddenly penetrated and the grin disappeared from his countenance. Damned if he hadn't been a bigger fool than she was! He moved over to stare out the narrow window, his glance as bleak as the rocky scene below.

When Carolyn reached her room, her disposition wasn't any better. She flung herself down in a chair and stared sadly at the cold fireplace.

Liz sauntered over to investigate the ancient lancet windows, but once she had made a token gesture of admiring the view she turned back. "All right, Caro. I'm still curious."

"Liz—I love you dearly, but even that doesn't give you and old Henry the right to pry in my private life."

Liz Sheppard accorded that pronouncement the brief derisive gesture it deserved. "Try saying it again and this time put more conviction in it, lamb."

"I'm twenty-five years old and . . ."

"And I'm on the shady side of forty-nine, so don't get on your high horse." She leaned comfortably against the wall. "Where did you find that man? I must say I like his type."

Carolyn stared at her. "I thought you were going to give me a lecture and you're acting like a designing widow."

"I *am* a designing widow, remember? So listen to your elders! A sprig like you should be married ... not getting caught in a man's bedroom dressed like that."

Carolyn put a hand to her forehead. "I can't tell whether you're chewing me out because I was in the bedroom or wearing three layers of clothes at the time."

Liz pushed her hair off her forehead and smiled at her. "I'm not sure myself. Fortunately now that I'm here, the situation won't recur. Even Mr. Evans would know better than to try issuing that invitation again."

Carolyn's cheeks flamed. "He didn't invite me," she said painfully. "If he had, I certainly wouldn't have gone."

"Let's start over. You've lost me somewhere along the way."

"I heard noises last night ... in the walls or under the floors or some place." She caught a glimpse of Liz's expression. "All right, laugh! There *were* noises, I tell you."

"So you weren't going to stay in here waiting until the ghost came through the wall and grabbed you."

"Very funny. You just wait until tonight. ..."

"My room's down the hall," Liz informed her.

"Not any more. It's in here," Caro said firmly. "Reese can bring in a cot or something for me and you can have the bed. Please, Liz, I *know* I heard something."

The other relented at Carolyn's urging. "Well, we'll see. I suppose we owe it to Henry to find out if his real estate comes complete with haunts." She waved a hand toward the window. "To be honest, I've seen more cheerful locales than this old castle. I didn't know it was perched on the edge of a cliff over that rocky shoreline."

Carolyn nodded with understanding. "All we need is a bloodhound howling and a nice eerie fog. Last night, Hugh called it a slight mist, but even he admitted that he prefers night life in London."

"I don't blame him. After those years in Rangoon, Lyonsgate Castle isn't the ideal holiday retreat for a man."

"You've met him?"

"This morning when I arrived at the crack of dawn. He was just setting out for his morning ride." She gave Carolyn a covert glance. "He's a nice-looking fellow. Not quite as rugged as your Michael but . . ."

"I keep telling you he is *not* my Michael! The man is merely a fellow American who rescued me from the roadside when my car conked out."

"In Wales?"

Carolyn stirred uncomfortably. "No . . . England," she admitted. "Actually he said he had some extra vacation time so he offered ..." She paused and then confessed, "I asked him to drive me here." The sight of Liz's face made her add hastily, "It was a strictly business proposition. That's why you were all wrong about our being together this morning. He has a girl back home. Some overblown Italian redhead called Gina."

"Your description or his?"

"Hardly his." Carolyn's lips tightened. "The man's absolutely dippy about her."

"Too bad. I liked his shoulders."

"So did ..." Carolyn caught herself and quickly changed the subject. "What's this about Hugh having a title?"

"Reese explained that he inherited unexpectedly after the presumed heir was killed in an automobile collision." Liz's tone was thoughtful. "Hugh made no bones about wanting to sell the castle—says he can't afford to keep it up."

"It is threadbare in parts," Carolyn admitted, "but there's enough silver in the drawing room alone to pay the taxes for a year."

"English gentry are inclined to think they're stony when they're down to their last Constable and Turner. I must say, though, that it isn't the place I'd choose for weekends."

"Then what do we tell Mr. Lyon?"

"Old Henry? We tell him the truth. He'd fire us both if he thought we had trumped up an excuse." She ran an appraising hand over the top of an oak chest. "However, it won't hurt if we list the heating bill and taxes first. He might as well know the worst straight away."

"How long will this job take?" Carolyn asked.

"Three or four days should do it. Why? Can't Michael stick around any longer?"

"He might ... if it doesn't conflict with the matches at Wimbledon. You'll have to ask him."

Liz picked up her purse and searched for a cigarette. "He doesn't look like a tennis bum. What else does he do?"

"I told you."

"I meant in addition to improving American-Italian relations." She used her lighter and then surveyed the younger woman. "I thought you were going to change for breakfast. You'd better get stirring."

"I know." Caro stood up wearily and went over to her suitcase. "Is there any hot water this early?"

"If hot water comes from what Reese called the geyser—then there is. For a minute, I thought he was talking about Yellowstone and Old Faithful." Liz moved over to flick a finger at the parcel in Carolyn's suitcase. "What did you buy?"

"A souvenir tile. Here—take a look. Mike ... er ... Mr. Evans bought it for me."

"It's all right . . . you can call him Mike." A dimple showed in Liz's cheek. "After all, we're all old friends."

"I don't know why I put up with you ... or

Henry," Carolyn said, throwing a navy blue and olive pantsuit over her arm. "Do you think Hugh approves of slacks at breakfast time?"

"We're interested in buying his castle and he's interested in selling," Liz said wryly, "so I imagine he'll approve. Besides, I gather you made quite an impression last night." She rewrapped the tile and put it carefully back in the suitcase. "I like your souvenir."

"It is nice, isn't it?" Carolyn paused at the threshold of the bathroom and asked suddenly, "Liz—have you ever seen a Sweetheart Spoon?"

"I don't think so." The other's attention was caught by the wistful note in Caro's voice. "Why? Did Mike buy one of those for you, too?"

"Of course not. I told you about his redhead ... he bought it for her."

"Then why do you ask ... ?" Liz broke off, shaking her head. "You're not making much sense this morning, my girl. I think something's addled your brains."

"Honestly, Liz ..." Carolyn gave her a despairing glance, "you don't understand at all."

Liz sat quietly on the bed staring at the bathroom door for some minutes after Carolyn closed it behind her. A faint frown creased her forehead and her eyes were soft with remembrance as she murmured, "Oh, but I do, my dear. I really do."

Chapter Six

Breakfast time took on the aspects of a good weekend house party. It was as if each participant had decided to be on his best behavior and the result was unexpectedly pleasant.

Carolyn was pleased to note a look of admiration on Hugh's face when he glimpsed her trim navy pants with a tunic of olive, white, and navy stripes topping a white sweater. Even Reese moved with alacrity to hold her chair at the long Jacobean refectory table. Michael stood politely while she was being seated although his glance had met hers only briefly as she came into the room with Liz.

The crackling fireplace fire at one end of the dining hall added another cheerful note to the atmosphere, helping to dispel the backdrop of leaden sky showing beyond the windows. Above them, historical battle flags in bright silken hues hung at intervals from the beamed cathedral ceiling, but the center of attention along one wall was an intricately carved oak sideboard which held massive silver serving dishes for the breakfast buffet.

From his place at the end of the table, Hugh was the urbane host. "Will you take coffee or tea with your breakfast?"

"Coffee at this point, thank you," Liz answered. "We both enjoyed our morning tea though. Do we help ourselves at the sideboard?"

"That's right. Come along and I'll show you the drill," Hugh said, moving over to lift one of the silver covers and glance inside. "There's fruit at this end—eggs and meat on down the line. Reese will bring your coffee. It's a good thing you two came when you did. Michael and I were about to collapse from starvation."

"It was all my fault," Carolyn confessed as she took up a dish for sliced peaches. "Please go on to your next course. Liz and I will catch up."

"Practically immediately," Liz confirmed, choosing pears over peaches.

"That's what I was hoping you'd say." Hugh lifted another silver cover further down the table. "What's it to be, Michael? rashers of bacon or frittered lamb's tongues?"

A serving spoon slipped from Mike's grasp and fell onto the table. "Sorry!" He bent to retrieve it and successfully avoided looking at the women's studiously blank faces. By the time he straightened, he was able to say, "The bacon . . . just two or three slices, please."

"Whatever you say," Hugh agreed. "You'll find Mrs. Reese an excellent cook and she offers quite a varied menu. Practically everything—except rice."

"Don't you like rice?" Carolyn asked him.

"After those years in Burma and four more to come in Hong Kong, I shudder when I see the stuff," Hugh said cheerfully. Then to Mike, "Scrambled eggs?"

"Thanks very much." The other extended his plate for a generous serving.

"There we are." Hugh enthusiastically heaped his plate with the lamb and shepherded them back to the table. "Here's Mrs. Reese with our toast."

Carolyn glanced curiously at the slight woman wearing a black serving dress who followed her husband into the room. Although her hair was white, her brows were still dark and matched her soulful deep-set eyes. Aside from the slight touch of red over her cheekbones, Mrs. Reese looked like a figure in a pencil sketch—consisting only of light and shadow. She kept her eyes averted as she put several filled toast racks along the table in front of them.

"Thank you, Mrs. Reese," Hugh said.

She merely bobbed her head at his automatic remark and hurried out of the room. As soon as her husband had filled their coffee cups and put the silver pot within reach, he followed her.

"I'm afraid you won't be able to have much of a conversation with Mrs. Reese," Hugh said apologetically. "She only speaks Welsh although she understands some English. Fortunately, Reese is usually around to help translate."

"Are they the only help in the castle?" Carolyn asked.

"There are some daily women for the rough cleaning and an occasional gardener." His voice was defensive. "Remember, most of Lyonsgate has been closed for years."

"Of course. I forgot for a minute that you just came home yourself."

"Calling this home sounds strange even now," he said ruefully. "One of the disadvantages of foreign service is that most of us feel like refugees when we're between assignments."

"I've heard that before," Mike told him, "from the British who lived and worked in Africa and Malaysia at the time of the colonies. It had been years since they had been back to England for more than a few weeks' leave."

Hugh sighed understandingly. "It's like the old saying—'we'll fight for England and die for her— but don't expect us to live in this bloody climate.'" He turned a bright glance on Liz and Carolyn. "That joke was laundered considerably for feminine ears."

Liz arrested her spoon halfway to her mouth. "I didn't *think* that was the original version."

"Getting back to the help here," Carolyn said with determination. "Are you sure Reese hasn't hired someone extra for a night shift?"

Hugh shook his head. "No ... I shouldn't think so. Why would he want anyone then?"

"Carolyn was concerned over some noises she heard last night," Mike put in smoothly. "It was shortly after we all went up to bed."

Hugh's thick eyebrows met in an ominous line. "I still don't understand. What kind of noises?"

"I can't explain very well ... sort of thumps and bumps," she said. "At first, I didn't think much of it, but the last time when I heard the groan ..."

There was a muffled crash behind them and they all turned to see Reese down on his knees retrieving some extra spoons from the floor. He glanced up, embarrassed. "I beg your pardon, Sir Hugh."

"Quite all right, Reese ... actually you arrived just in time. Miss Drummond mentioned some noises in the night. Did you hear anything?"

Reese stood up with some difficulty and put his head to one side as he concentrated. "I can't think what it could have been, Miss. Mind you, the wind from the sea causes a whistling around the windows."

Carolyn began to wish that she had never mentioned the subject.

Reese fixed his gaze on Mike. "Did you hear anything, sir?"

"No." The word came out reluctantly. "Nothing at all."

Liz saw Caro's miserable expression and broke in. "Old buildings always creak in strange ways. I'm sure our Mr. Lyon would be intrigued at the idea of secret tunnels. Don't all castles have a priest's hole or hidden passages?"

Hugh reached for the marmalade. "That idea isn't far off. We still have a trough for pouring the boiling oil over one of the lintels in Lyonsgate, but I think our last tunnel was boarded up about the turn of the century. Isn't that right, Reese?"

"Yes, sir. If you'll remember, it was after the last outbreak of smuggling in these parts."

"Then there *was* a tunnel!" Carolyn exclaimed.

"Oh yes, Miss Drummond." Reese carefully arranged the spoons on his tray. "It led from the west wing of the castle down to the beach. Of course, after fire destroyed that part of the castle, the tunnel was put out of commission. The year was 1908, wasn't it, Sir Hugh?"

"You're the expert." Hugh took a sip of his coffee. "I'm sorry, Carolyn, but ghosts would have a hard time haunting Lyonsgate these days. The only official haunt fairly close by is in Caerphilly Castle."

"That's right, Sir Hugh," Reese confirmed,

nodding. "She was a French princess who lived in the castle at the time of Henry II. They call her the Green Lady."

"What happened to her?" Liz wanted to know.

Reese pursed his lips thoughtfully. "Her husband sent her back to France after she fell in love with a Welsh prince named Tew Teg. After her death abroad, they say she came back to reclaim her true love."

"But apparently the lovers had a bit of trouble getting together," Hugh put in, "because the Green Lady is still wandering about Caerphilly centuries later. We've nothing as romantic here in Lyonsgate, I'm afraid. All I can do is show you the secret of our family chapel and where my ancestors hid the family jewels—when there were any left to hide," he added bitterly.

"There you are, Carolyn ... you'll have your mystery after all," Liz said, trying to lighten the atmosphere. "I have a question too, Reese. I'd like to know how your wife gets this wonderful flavor in her canned fruit. Does she add a touch of ginger in the preserving?"

"I'll have to ask her, Mrs. Sheppard," the old man beamed. "I'm sure Helen would give you the recipe if you'd like it."

"I would ... definitely! And I'll come down to the kitchen after breakfast to track it down. If that's all right with you, Hugh?"

"Of course. Feel free to wander as you please. You can inspect all the skeletons in the family closets if it will help persuade your employer. Reese will answer any questions you have."

"I'll be pleased to, Sir Hugh." The retainer edged back to the pantry door. "If there's nothing else, sir . . ."

"Just make sure the chapel is unlocked so I can show Miss Drummond through after breakfast."

"I'll look after it right away, sir."

"Well, that takes care of three of us," Liz said as the door swung closed behind him. "What are you going to do after breakfast, Mike?"

"There are a couple of telephone calls I should make."

"Use the phone in my study," Hugh said. "There's plenty of privacy there."

"I suppose you're checking on your tickets for the tennis tournament," Carolyn put in scathingly. She was still smarting from his parting remark in the bedroom and decided it wouldn't hurt to point out what a useless life he led.

"That might be a good idea," he said blandly. "Thanks for reminding me." He turned to Hugh. "Miss Drummond knows I'm planning on Wimbledon."

"Don't tell me you've managed tickets!" The other hunched forward in his chair. "What splendid luck! Mind you, I don't think the Aussie has a chance against the Frenchman unless he gets two quick sets. . . ."

Immediately the two men entered into a heated discussion of the forthcoming tennis tournament that left both women stranded on the conversational sidelines. Only the amused glance Mike gave Carolyn as she finally nudged him to pass the cream made her aware that he didn't need the sports page of a newspaper to bypass her completely.

As for Hugh, she knew from his engrossed expression that he had even forgotten about his invitation to the chapel.

Liz reached over to pour more coffee and whisper, "It's all right, Caro—we can always swoon when we get up from the table and get their attention that way. But take some advice from an elderly widow, dear. Never, never bring up the subject of sporting events when you're with a man. Probably even Venus de Milo was left standing on her pedestal when the Greek wrestling matches were scheduled."

Carolyn sipped her cold coffee and seethed in silence. Liz was right! But if the Venus was left unattended at a Greek orgy, it was undoubtedly because one of Mike Evans' ancestors had a ticket for the relay races the same night.

Finally, in desperation, Carolyn pushed back her chair, murmured a brief excuse and abruptly left the table. Fortunately, Hugh remembered his duties as a host before she reached the stairway.

He caught her elbow, still winded from his

chase. "I *am* sorry, Carolyn. It was so relaxing to talk with a chap without being diplomatic for a change. Mike certainly does know his tennis."

"Then don't let me disturb you," she said easily.

"Now don't *you* be silly." He lightly drew his finger down the inside of her forearm and smiled at her involuntary response. "There were other things I missed in Burma too," he said conversationally. "A hell of a lot more than tennis matches." His smile deepened as she flushed and made a feeble attempt to draw her arm away. "Come on." He led the way to the heavy front door. "Let's inspect the chapel and talk about really important things."

Carolyn's first impression of the chapel wing was one of unstinted admiration. Although the passing years and financial hardships had dimmed the grandeur in other parts of the castle, the chapel reflected a glory heightened by its long history.

The rich tones of the stained glass windows on the side walls and behind the altar threw a strong assortment of colors on the slate floor and the family pews. The walls were enhanced with the lovely patina of oak paneling and the wood was repeated in the ancient kneeling benches. In front of them on the altar, a fine linen cloth lay under the intricately chased silver cross which occupied the place of honor.

"It's perfectly beautiful," Carolyn told Hugh

in a hushed voice. She fingered a worn tapestry kneeling pad hooked onto the back of a pew. "Do you still hold services here?"

He nodded. "The local vicar includes it in his rounds and the villagers come for certain Saint's days."

She smiled faintly. "I'm impressed, I really am! I've never known anyone who had a private chapel before."

"Don't go by appearances. Unless your millionaire employer has a yearning for *his* own private chapel, I'll be absolutely skint trying to pay the taxes this year. The death duties on the estate have cleansed the coffers. Of course, I could sell some of the land but . . ." He broke off and ran his fingers through his hair. "It's a terrible responsibility."

"You could always marry a wealthy wife," she said in a light tone.

His face brightened. "So I could. How are your finances?"

"Sorry . . . I'd have trouble paying your vicar's salary." She rifled through the pages of a leather-backed hymnal. "No girl next door?"

"Not exactly . . ."

"Nor anywhere else?" There was genuine interest in her face.

He grinned. "You Americans don't beat around the brush. . . ."

"Bush," she corrected.

"Bush, then. All right, if you really want to

127

know—there's a good friend in Scotland with lots of lovely lolly."

Carolyn wasn't sure what "lovely lolly" meant, but it sounded negotiable. "Well?"

He shook his head slowly but definitely. "No thank you. I'd end up working for Sylvia's father in his biscuit factory. Sylvia might not wear the trousers in our family, but he definitely would. It would never work." He rubbed his hand gently across the top of a pew. "I'll find another way to live before going to a woman with my cap in hand."

"If she loved you, it wouldn't matter."

"It would to me." British reserve was evident in every clipped syllable. "Enough of that. I promised to show you the family cache too. You see that carving in the oak at the base of the altar?"

Carolyn followed him down the main aisle to peer curiously where he pointed. "The reference to Proverbs xxvi, verse xiii?"

"That's the one. Well, a few hundred years ago one of my Lyon ancestors took that verse literally."

"Wait a minute. You'll have to educate me. What *is* the twenty-sixth proverb?"

"Sorry," his smile flashed. "I forgot most people wouldn't know. That particular verse reads 'there is a lion in the way; a lion is in the streets.' When one of the sieges hit the castle, my early relatives chose to use the lion fountain by the front door as a repository for the family jewels and carved that verse as the key. They reasoned that in the years to come, someone would interpret the clue and check 'all the lions on the way' if they were still searching for the family baubles."

Carolyn's eyes glistened with excitement. "Did they ever find the jewels?"

"Oh yes. The cache was discovered a couple of hundred years ago, so there's no use looking these days." He scratched the top of his nose thoughtfully. "As a matter of fact, there's even an epigram carved at the base of the fountain now. I think my grandfather was responsible for that—in case any future generations thought there might be some treasure still tucked away."

"What does the epigram say?"

"It comes from Martial and translated means 'Don't pluck the beard of a dead lion.'" He looked down on her wryly. "In other words, don't count on any more loot. It was sold to patch the castle roof a long time ago."

She strolled by his side back to the chapel door. "At least your ancestors had a sense of humor."

"It's difficult to eat on that alone." He ushered her outside and then turned to close and lock the heavy wooden door. "I'd like to extend our tour, but I promised to see one of the tenant farmers about now. He needs some repairs done to his cottage."

"Of course—go right ahead." Carolyn glanced

at her watch. "If you don't mind, I'll wander for a while. This fresh air smells marvelous and I don't think the rain will hold off much longer."

Hugh glanced upward. "I daresay you're right. You'd best stay fairly close."

She nodded. "Don't worry about me. I'll just poke my nose over the edge of the cliff so I can see your beach properly."

"Good enough . . ." he hesitated before striding away. "Watch the path down the side of the hill. Sometimes the loose shale sifts from the rocks above and makes the going difficult until it's cleared away."

"I'll be careful." She returned his casual wave and watched him take the path back toward a side entrance to the castle. Then she sniffed the salt air happily and turned to meander past the outer wall of the chapel, picking her way carefully through the rock-strewn ground.

In one spot there was a partial circle of stones surrounding a rough mound and she wondered if it was one of the cromlechs or stone burial chambers that she had read about in Welsh history. She shivered slightly, not quite sure whether it was caused by the sudden gust of wind or the thought of that harsh graveside scene. Even in death, the Welsh seemed to favor the sterner elements.

Her steps slowed as she approached the edge of the grayish-black cliff which extended all the way to the foundation of the castle itself. The path wound past two good-sized boulders and she moved over to them, standing for a moment to stare at the panorama beneath.

The steep drop of the rugged rib of rock made her catch her breath. All along the cliff, stone spurs covered with patches of wild thyme held the rough hillside back from the turbulent bay waters below.

Directly in front of her, the path wound down the hillside in switchback pattern. She craned over the edge to see where it finally emerged on the partially sheltered beach. Once again there was the study in contrasts which typified the Welsh countryside; at high tide level there were ragged rock arches under the cliff, but they stood right next to a strip of peaceful sandy beach. Farther to the right, three immense boulders studded the water's edge and caused the sea to foam as it surged around them.

Over her head, the white body of a spectral gull rode the quickening breeze like a weekend glider pilot. His mournful cry was the only diversion in an almost oppressive silence.

It would be nice, Carolyn thought suddenly, to see someone strolling along that beach or to hear shrill childish voices—anything to add a touch of normality. This way, it was as if she were the only human being within hundreds of miles. She shivered again and pulled her jacket collar up for extra warmth.

As she started to turn back toward the chapel, a

small fishing vessel rounded the end of a rock spine which protruded into the sea immediately to her right. The muddy green boat was about thirty feet long and even at that distance looked weather-worn and in need of a dry dock session.

Carolyn lifted her hand to shade her eyes and strained to catch a glimpse of the crew. She saw a sudden flash and knew instinctively that she was being watched by an unseen helmsman with a pair of binoculars. Her lips went up in a reluctant smile. It was like peering through a keyhole only to discover an intent eye on the other side of the door peering right back.

As she watched, the boat cut its power and bobbed aimlessly on the swells. Evidently the captain was unsure of his course. If he came much closer inshore, she decided, he'd find trouble in the currents around those rocks.

Moving strictly by instinct, she started down the path to the beach. From a lower level, she could discover if the fishing boat was truly without power and if she could help in any way to keep it from running aground.

She reached the first switchback in the steep path and slowed to get around the narrow turn. If she didn't watch out, she'd be down on the beach considerably sooner than she had planned. Obviously a person only took a shortcut once on that steep rock precipice. If he survived the descent, the trip back to the top would be on a stretcher. At that sobering thought, she even forgot the fishing boat for a moment as she concentrated on the narrow walkway.

Her eyes took in the spectacle of small rocks and gravel striking the path around her before her mind fully grasped the danger. Even then she didn't realize the consequences of the ominous grating and slithering noises above her head.

She simply stopped and looked up to see what appeared to be the entire surface of the hillside coming down upon her.

Her scream shattered the stillness as the main force hit her. She sprawled at full length on the path, trying desperately to stay under the rocky overhang. Heavy stone fragments and gravel pelted her arms which were thrust up to protect her head. In the middle of the onslaught, one sharp piece of shale caught a glancing blow behind her ear which made her gasp with sudden pain. After that she closed her eyes and lost track of time.

Then abruptly it was over. The last rocks crashed down onto the beach and the final remnants of gravel dust filtered over her fallen figure. Slowly, painfully, Carolyn pushed herself erect.

There was a warm trickle coursing down the side of her neck. She put up a curious hand and brought down red-streaked fingers. Still dazed, she groped futilely for a handkerchief.

Her thoughts churned chaotically although physically she still moved in slow motion. A brief spasm of dizziness made her scrabble nervously at the cliffside beside her and she shook her head to clear it.

Oh lord, she thought, the man on the fishing boat will think I've gone mad. She rubbed her eyes with dusty fists and then peered out toward the water to see if he had emerged from the boat's cabin during her trouble.

There was only the unbroken expanse of restless gray water in front of her. Like the fabled Loch Ness monster, the fishing boat had disappeared completely.

Carolyn blinked her eyes once . . . twice . . . and then looked at the empty water again. Surely she wasn't suffering from hallucinations as well as shock! She took a faltering step backward as her glance went up the cliff above her to find the start of the avalanche path—almost afraid she had imagined that as well.

There, on the crest of the crag looking like a brooding Bernini statue carved out of the blackened stone, stood Mike Evans staring down at her.

Chapter Seven

Illusion shortly succumbed to reality.

Carolyn opened her eyes a minute later and found Michael bending over her where she had again collapsed on the path.

"Don't try to move!" There was a firm arm around her shoulders and his voice was anxious. "Are you all right?"

"I'm perfectly fine," she said, stubbornly getting to her feet. "It was just the shock of seeing you up there. You didn't start that landslide deliberately, did you?"

"What are you talking about?" He stared at her. "What landslide?"

"Then I guess you didn't. Nobody would be stupid enough to stand there and wait to be discovered."

"Let's get you out of here. You probably hit your head when you fainted just now." He was pulling a handkerchief from his pocket as he spoke.

"I didn't faint . . . exactly. I told you. It was the surprise of seeing you."

"My lord, you've seen me before!"

"Not after a rock shower has just crashed over me." She took the handkerchief from him and dabbed behind her ear. "That's when I collected this lump."

He brushed some grit from her shoulders and eyed her uneasily. "What makes you think someone was responsible for it?"

"Because it was too coincidental. Don't look at me as if I'm going out of my mind." She pushed his hand away irritably.

"I'm not doing anything of the kind."

"You certainly are."

Mike decided it would be therapeutic to change the subject.

He took the handkerchief from her and mopped the dirt from her cheeks. "Pipe down or I *will* think you've scrambled your brains." He started to dust the top of her nose and then stopped. "What d'ya know? They don't come off— they're freckles. Five of them. I thought they went out with Queen Victoria."

Her head jerked up. "Very funny. And there are only four."

He concentrated on counting. "You're right . . . four it is. The fifth one *is* dirt." He flicked the handkerchief lightly. "Now everything's back to normal." There was the merest glance at the cut behind her ear before he said casually, "Put your arms around my neck."

"Whatever for?"

"Because I'm carrying you back to the castle." He lifted her easily and started up the path.

"This isn't necessary," she said with a total lack of conviction. When he didn't bother to answer, she relaxed and burrowed her head into his shoulder. It felt wonderful to be held so securely against that strong body. Suddenly she discovered that in addition to her throbbing headache, her breathing apparatus was out of whack too. Hopefully Michael couldn't hear her heart pounding away in double time against his chest . . . or could he? It would certainly be safer to put a good distance between them before he found out. She started struggling to get down, saying, "I can walk by myself. . . ."

"Dammit . . . hang on, will you! It's a long way to the bottom of this rock pile."

Hastily she wound her arms more tightly around his neck. "I know it."

"Then what were you doing down here in the first place?"

"I was watching a boat. . . ."

"Can't you watch boats from the top of the cliff?"

"Not this one." She glanced past his stubborn jaw and added defensively, "It was so close to shore that I thought they might be in trouble, so

I started down the path. Then the heavens let loose raining rocks."

"Was that when you screamed?"

"I guess so." Unconsciously she edged closer.

His clasp tightened but his expression didn't change. He merely said, "I heard you when I was wandering around the chapel. It took a while to find you."

"You didn't see anyone up there?"

"Nary a soul." He shifted her in his arms as they reached the top of the cliff.

"I'm too heavy," she said remorsefully. "You'd better put me down. I can walk ... honestly I can."

He ignored her request. "Don't be a nuisance. Now that we're on the level, you're a feather in the breeze.

"I won't be if I keep eating those cheese and tomato sandwiches." She plucked his handkerchief from his shirt pocket and dabbed at her neck where the blood was inching down in a tiny rivulet. "Damn! I hope this won't get on your shirt."

"I'm not worried. Try to keep as quiet as possible."

"I will." Reaction was beginning to set in and she sighed wearily. "One miserable fishing boat— even a disappearing one—wasn't worth this."

Mike opened his mouth to question her further and then noted her drooping eyes. "Forget it. In five more minutes, you'll be tucked in that monstrosity of a bed."

Her lids raised the slightest bit. "No Poppa Bear this time?"

"He only pays sick calls later in the day. We'll wait and see what the doctor says about visitors."

Liz met them in the main hall, took over with a minimum of fuss and a maximum of efficiency. Carolyn was deposited in her bed forthwith. It was a warmed bed this time with a hot water bottle at her feet and one to clutch in her chilled hands. Reese called the doctor while Michael and Hugh hovered uncertainly in the hallway.

"Perhaps some brandy ..." Hugh suggested when Liz finally joined them.

"I think that's a very good idea," she agreed, "but for you and Mike. Reese said the doctor was just starting out on his rounds so he should be here shortly. I believe we should wait for him to prescribe for Carolyn," she added gently.

"Of course ... whatever you say." Hugh thrust his hands deep in his pockets. "I feel terrible about this. There's never been any trouble on that path before ... has there, Reese?" He turned to confront the manservant, who approached carrying a tray of tea things.

Reese had lost his usual air of imperturbability. Probably, Liz thought shrewdly, because it was difficult to cope with an influx of houseguests after months of undisturbed caretaking.

Hugh was going on, "At least you didn't write about any rock slides."

"I wasn't aware the surface was loose, Sir Hugh," Reese confirmed unhappily. "Possibly it's because we've had so much rain this spring."

"That could have a lot to do with it," Mike put in diplomatically. "Is that refreshment for us, Reese?"

"Would you care for tea, Mr. Evans?"

Mike grinned. "Only if there's nothing else offered."

Hugh brightened immediately. "Consider it offered. I think we need that medicinal brandy."

"I'll have tea, thanks," Liz told Reese, opening the bedroom door for him. "It sounds like just the thing while we're waiting for the doctor."

Hugh caught at her arm before she went back in the room. His voice was pitched low so that it wouldn't reach the bed. "Do you think Carolyn is seriously hurt?"

"I don't believe so. Right now, she's getting over the shock of a frightening experience. When you remember she had a rather unsettled time last night ..." her eyes flicked thoughtfully at Mike's still figure ..." she's more vulnerable than usual, that's all."

"I hope you're right," Hugh told her.

"So do I. Thank goodness there's an expert on the way." She turned to Mike and said, "You look as if you're a little under the weather too. Maybe the doctor should make two calls."

140

"Forget it!" He interrupted her ruthlessly. "Carolyn's the only patient. Hugh and I will send the doctor up as soon as he arrives." He turned and strode down the hall, his steps echoing on the stone floor.

Hugh glanced at Liz, lifted his hands in a humorous shrug, and followed.

"Will that be all, Mrs. Sheppard?" Reese hovered beside her.

"Yes, thanks—for the moment. I imagine the gentlemen need you more than I do."

He looked after their disappearing figures. "Was Mr. Evans hurt as well?"

"Not where it shows," she replied briskly. "Do you think they'll remember to eat lunch after their therapeutic brandy?"

"Don't worry, madam," he promised. "I shall make sure they do."

For Carolyn, the rest of the day passed in a pleasant haze.

When the doctor arrived, he turned out to be a pleasant young man in his early thirties who boasted a thick Scottish accent and cheerfully admitted he was a displaced resident of Edinburgh. Americans, he confided to Carolyn while unobtrusively taking her pulse, were a frail lot like the English.

"Now a Scotsman wouldna' feel a thing when the stones came showerin' doon."

"Why not?" Caro mumbled around the thermometer he put in her mouth.

141

"Thick heads, lass," he said, tapping his cranium. "Verra thick heads." He leaned over to prop up her eyelid with a gentle thumb and then retrieved the thermometer. Giving it a casual glance he said, "Ye'll noo be goin' to see the funeral furnisher yet awhile." He switched abruptly to very good English. "That's what we call the undertaker over here. I feel obliged to translate for you colonials."

From her post by the window, Liz returned his friendly grin. "Very kind of you. The patient will live, I take it."

"Yes indeed." He rummaged in his black bag and pulled out a glass phial. "Quite comfortably if she takes two of these pills every four hours for the rest of the day." He shook the capsules into his palm and then into an envelope which he left on the bed table.

"Can't I get up?" Carolyn asked.

"Not if you're my patient," he told her sternly. "Bed rest until tomorrow morning. Give that lump of yours time to subside." He held out two of the pills and watched her swallow them with a sip of water. The movement made her wince and he nodded understandingly. "Those will help the pain as well."

"As well as what?"

He snapped his bag closed. "As well as giving you a nice sleep. I'll call in tomorrow. Don't bother to see me out," he told Liz. "I blazed a

142

trail on my way up here. Now I'd better get home to report to my wife."

"What do you mean?"

He shrugged into a worn topcoat which he had dropped on a chair by the door. "She'll want to hear about the inside of the castle. Most of us in the village have never had the first look in. The caretaker . . . Reese, is it? . . . took his duties verra seriously. Unless that nephew of his was visiting, the gates were kept locked."

"Reese probably felt it was his duty while Sir Hugh was away," Liz said.

"Maybe." The doctor's tone was politely dubious. "Anyway, it's nice to see the old place come to life again. All of us in the village hope Sir Hugh will stay around a bit." He glanced at his watch and hurriedly opened the door. "I'll check with you tomorrow. Miss Drummond should be feeling much better by then."

Miss Drummond did.

Miss Drummond also slept through the day as if she had been clubbed. When nighttime came, all of Cromwell's army could have marched behind the walls of the castle and she wouldn't have heard them.

The next forenoon, it was the sound of voices which caused her to open her eyes and rejoin the world.

Threads of pale sunlight crisscrossed her blanket as she pushed up on an elbow and tried a vertical position. Other than feeling a slight giddiness which quickly passed, she decided she was practically as good as new—certainly well enough to get out of bed and find something to eat.

Cheerful bursts of laughter floated up to her opened window and she padded over to discover what was happening. She had to flatten her nose against the pane and peer downward before she could see Liz and Mike standing by the rear of a milk delivery truck. From their charadelike actions, it appeared that Liz was trying to buy something from the brawny driver, who was rummaging in the back of the van.

Another spate of laughter came after the purchase when Liz searched her pockets and discovered that she had no money with her. She made an emptyhanded gesture and appealed to Mike, who obligingly took out his wallet.

Carolyn felt as if she were watching a stage play from the second balcony when a picture fell from his billfold and Liz bent over to pick it up. The older woman glanced at it and then slowly handed it back. From her expression, she was obviously teasing Mike about it but he made short work of his explanation and tucked his prize carefully back in his wallet.

Caro tried to get a better look before it disappeared, but only succeeded in bumping her nose painfully on the window. Naturally, Mike took that moment to look up and recognize her. She belatedly remembered her uncombed hair plus her mussed pajamas and hurriedly retired from view. Unfortunately not before Liz and the milk-man stared upward as well.

It was one thing to be caught unawares in a diaphanous negligee, quite another to be surprised in striped flannel pajamas with a strip of adhesive tape hanging over one's ear.

"Damn!" muttered Carolyn forcefully. "Damn, damn, damn!"

Even the sight of Poppa Bear's molting figure in front of her fireplace did little to raise her morale. At that moment, she looked as bad as he did.

Doctor's orders or not—it was time to take positive steps.

A warm bath helped her spirits. So did the donning of a fiery red knit dress with a broad middy collar and a clinging pleated skirt. She stepped into a pair of burnished dark brown pumps that were neither sensible nor comfortable but were immensely flattering to her trim ankles and legs.

"Who wants to walk for miles?" she murmured, well pleased with the result.

Even her hair behaved for a change and made a glistening camouflage for the lump behind her ear. The doctor's bandage had been changed for two discreet band-aids which didn't show at all. She took a last look in the wavy mirror mounted by a Lyon ancestor on the back of the bathroom door and sailed confidently out into the bedroom.

Liz was pouring a cup of tea from the tray on

the bed table. "I thought I timed this about right," she said calmly. "Should you be up and dressed?"

Carolyn took the cup that she held out and said, "I'm fine. Heavens I shouldn't have to sleep again for a month." She sipped the steaming liquid cautiously. "What was so funny down on the drive with the milkman?"

"At Lyonsgate Castle, you don't get delivery from a milkman," Liz said. "That young man was called Jack the Milk and it's a social occasion when he calls. I wanted some of that wonderful cream—you know the kind—where it's so thick it scarcely pours."

"Think of the calories. . . ."

"*You* think of the calories," Liz told her. "I'll think of something else. My lord, a body has to look forward to something after a breakfast of steamed bloaters and caraway waffles."

"You're kidding!"

The other raised her hand. "True, so help me. The sacrifices I make for Henry Lyon would never be believed. Whatever happened to those famous Welsh trout they're supposed to grill for breakfast?"

"Maybe Mrs. Reese wants to speed us on our way."

"Well, she's certainly succeeding. Incidentally she wondered what you'd like for breakfast."

"*Not* steamed bloaters and caraway . . ."

"I know, I know," Liz interrupted. "I've already ordered scrambled eggs. Enough for the two of us, I hope." She poured herself a cup of tea. "Hugh asked if you'd feel like lunch down on the beach. That's if the weather holds," she added hastily. "This place reminds me of Ireland, where they tell you, 'it's a foine day' at ten-thirty and the rain is pouring down at eleven."

Carolyn nodded. "I'm suspicious whenever I see green grass in a country any more."

"With good reason," the other agreed. "These Welsh are certainly rugged optimists. Do you know that Reese suggested I take my swimming costume down at lunch? Stop giggling! Those were his exact words. 'Swimming costume' in this weather! Now a fur coat would make sense."

"I've been thinking about that," Carolyn mused. "Do you honestly think old Henry will want to spend his summers here? The damp air won't help his arthritis one bit."

Liz chewed on her lower lip. "For a hardhead-ed business man, Henry can be amazingly illogi-cal. I think it tickled his vanity to dream of own-ing his namesake's castle and little things like climate and plumbing didn't make a dent."

"Can you convince him differently? Perhaps we're here under false pretenses. . . . I mean, Hugh's been nice about everything and he wants to sell the castle so badly but. . . ."

"Our first loyalty is to Henry. Yes, I know. I think all we can do is make an honest report. The true facts on this place would stagger anyone—

147

even a millionaire." She put her cup and saucer back on the tray. "Frankly, my guess is that Henry's merely testing the water, but he has no intention of plunging in."

"Then shouldn't we tell Hugh?"

"Tell him what? This is just educated guesswork on my part. I could drop a few discreet hints, though."

"That would help." Absently Carolyn scuffed the toe of her shoe along the bear rug.

Liz noted the movement. "Are you getting attached to that creature? When Michael brought it along last night, I thought he was out of his mind. Now I'm not so sure."

"He was probably trying to be funny. Actually he looks much better when the temperature goes down and you need some extra warmth."

"Are you talking about Michael or the bear?"

"Honestly Liz—that steamed bloater has gone to your head."

"I wish it had—rather than my stomach." Liz sighed and sat down on the edge of the bed. "There's a lot to be said for boiled eggs."

"Maybe you'd better rest if you don't feel well. A beach lunch is awful unless you're definitely in the mood."

Liz looked around the room and shuddered. "I don't want to stay up here by myself and conversation with Mrs. Reese leaves a lot to be desired. I got more response from that white cat of hers than anyone else in the family."

148

"Then I'll stay with you. . . ."

"It isn't necessary." Her smile was gentle. "I appreciate the offer, sweetie, but that tea made me feel better. By lunchtime, I'll be back to normal and the fresh air will be good for both of us. Remember, though, there's no leaping up and down that path for you until the doctor gives his approval. He should be here shortly."

Carolyn snapped her fingers. "Poof! A mere formality . . . I feel fine. Maybe I'll get another glimpse of my fishing boat when we're down on the beach."

Liz glanced up. "Do they fish out in the bay?"

"I guess so. Remind me to ask Hugh?" She went over to sit beside the older woman and give her an affectionate hug. "Thanks for being so sweet and taking care of me yesterday. I *am* glad you're along on this trip."

"Stuff!" Liz stirred in embarrassment. "Of course I'd take care of you. Did you think I'd turn you over to Mrs. Reese? And as for coming along . . ." Her cheeks creased with laughter. "My father once said—'Liz would go to hell if somebody would just invite her.'"

Carolyn giggled. "Well, today you have to take all invitations in turn and Hugh got his in first."

Liz couldn't argue with that logic, so by one o'clock she and Carolyn were on the beach following Hugh's instructions.

"You two women anchor the corners of that plastic tarp and then you can relax until we're

149

ready to eat. Mike . . . you'd best store the coffee flask and the bottle of wine over by that rock." Hugh put down a big wicker hamper with relief. "I think Mrs. Reese put some rocks in this bloody thing—it's that heavy."

"Reese said something about furnishing enough food for teatime, as well," Mike reminded him after putting down his burdens and coming back to stand over them. Dressed in a heavy roll-neck fisherman's sweater and a pair of casual slacks, he fitted easily into the rugged background.

Carolyn followed his glance along the beach which showed gravel patches in the sand near the cliffs. North of them, a long stone finger reached into the sea. It was behind that, she decided, that her fishing boat had disappeared yesterday.

Her gaze moved back toward the bottom of the cliff behind it and she noted a rock arch which evidently filled with water at high tide.

"Is that a sea cave over there?" she asked Hugh, pointing in its direction.

"Quite right. This whole coastline is dotted with them. It made things handy when smuggling was in vogue with the local residents. Reese could tell you about that. I've forgotten the exact story, but I think some of his relatives were involved at one time. My mother told me about it years ago."

"What did they smuggle?"

"French brandy and wines. Velvets and laces for their ladies. Anything they could turn a profit on." He grimaced comically. "My relatives undoubtedly took part too. Unfortunately, their good brandy disappeared years ago."

"The kind you served yesterday wasn't mediocre," Mike said.

"Not too bad," Hugh admitted. "My French relatives keep me supplied even today." He intercepted a suspicious look from Liz. "It's strictly legal, so don't start writing anonymous notes to the tax collector."

She grinned lazily. "I wouldn't think of it."

Carolyn was still staring down the beach. "Can a person go in the caves around here?"

He looked up from unfastening the picnic hamper. "If you want to. There's not much to recommend them. . . . They're damp and moldy for the most part. Difficult to move around in, too." His voice was abstracted as he searched through the contents of the basket. "Lunch looks better than usual. Mike, sit down and we'll serve the ladies." He was lifting out plates and napkins. "I told Mrs. Reese that all Americans liked sandwiches, so there should be a stack of those. Ah . . . here they are." He pulled one apart to check the filling. "These are fish paste. . . ."

The three Americans stared at each other with carefully blank faces.

"What other kind is there?" Liz asked finally in her most polite tone.

"Looks like . . ." Hugh huddled over the hamper. "Yes, it *is* . . . cheese and tomato."

Mike had trouble controlling his voice. "Carolyn's favorite. She mentioned it the other day."

"Really!" Hugh was plainly delighted.

Carolyn looked at the fish paste and decided to be thankful. "Absolutely," she said, "and I'm simply starved."

Despite their apprehensions, the lunch was varied and tasty. In addition to sandwiches, there was a delicious cheddar cheese which Hugh served with thin slices of succulent York ham. Dessert was a Welsh version of apple tart called Apple Amber made from a recipe dating back to 1700. Mrs. Reese had put it in individual serving dishes and, along with steaming coffee, it tasted unbelievably good.

Mike rearranged himself against the boulder he was using as a back rest and lit a cigarette. He took a look at the peaceful scene around them and said to Hugh, "You're out of your mind to want to sell all this. It's so quiet it's like living in another world."

"Sometimes I think you're right." Hugh sniffed the tangy salt air appreciatively. "Mind you, the place is more attractive with you people around than when the Reeses and I were rattling about by ourselves."

Liz scraped a spoon carefully around her dish to get the last bite of dessert. "Your problem's solved then," she told him. "I could get used to being a professional houseguest here. Even Mrs. Reese's cooking is growing on me." She looked ruefully down at her stocky figure. "Especially around the waistline."

"You couldn't spare a pound," Hugh assured her. "Seriously, I hope you will stay as long as you can. Your presence must have inspired Mrs. Reese. She was so unstrung over her cat's disappearance this morning that I thought we'd only get cold sausage rolls for lunch."

"I *did* mention that I was anxious to try some real Welsh food when I saw her yesterday." Liz reached over and tucked the empty dish in the hamper. "You mean that pretty white cat of hers has disappeared?"

He nodded.

"Why the panic?" Mike asked. "Cats keep their own schedules, don't they?" He saw Carolyn's skeptical expression. "Look, I don't claim to be an expert on the subject, but a friend of mine is a cat fancier and she complains her tomcat is out . . . er . . . visiting . . . half the time."

Caro frowned and glanced away. Obviously Gina's cat had the moral habits of his mistress and Mike observed both with tolerant amusement. Or, worse still, tacit approval.

"Just try explaining that theory to Mrs. Reese," Hugh was saying. "Since she doesn't have any children to worry about, she lavishes all her attention on that cat. If he's five minutes late for his breakfast kipper, she's out on the headlands looking for him. Even old Reese can't do anything with her."

"S'funny . . . she doesn't look like the type to flap," Liz commented. "Most of these Welsh women are so quiet. Generations and generations of them go on caring for the same belongings and living in the same towns as their ancestors."

"Maybe she just likes her cat," Mike said calmly.

Liz turned to him with a sheepish smile. "You're probably right. Here I am . . . acting like a weekend psychiatrist."

"You should have been with me in Burma," Hugh said. "A psychiatrist could have set up a practice with our wonderful collection of characters. The head of my section had retreated from the world, but unfortunately, it followed him. He solved that problem by only appearing for work once a week."

"Didn't his bosses find out?" Carolyn asked.

Hugh leaned over to pour more coffee. "It was difficult for anyone to check on him. You see, we celebrated our own holidays and then we had to celebrate the national Burmese holidays as well—plus their religious festivals. It was sometimes confusing to know when you were on duty. One month we only worked four days out of thirty."

Her mouth fell open. "You're kidding!"

"I'm not."

"If you ever need two more secretaries, let us know," Liz told him.

"Or a handyman to dust the desk tops," Mike put in.

Hugh held up his hands in surrender. "Remember, I've been transferred to Hong Kong. We'll probably work fourteen hours a day there." He noted their skeptical faces and compromised, "Well, at least eight. I'll let you know. Of course, if your Mr. Lyon buys the family homestead, I could stay in London and live off the loot."

Carolyn and Liz shared a glance. Then the older woman stirred uncomfortably, saying, "Look Hugh, don't count on it. Henry has had eccentric ideas before."

He reached over and patted her shoulder. "Don't worry, Liz. Frankly, I can't imagine even an American millionaire wanting a financial drain like Lyonsgate." He put his empty mug in the hamper and stood up. "Who's for a walk down the beach? I've eaten so much that I need some exercise."

"I'd like to . . ." Carolyn started to say but Liz interrupted.

"No, you don't, my girl. The doctor told you to take it easy today. Remember?"

"I'd forgotten . . . honestly." Caro settled back again. "Sorry, Hugh. Let me take a rain check."

Mike got up beside him. "I'll volunteer. I've been wanting to take a look down at the south end of the beach."

"Good." Hugh turned. "Liz, what about you?"

"I'm stuffed with good intentions but absolutely devoid of energy. A nap sounds better to me. Carolyn and I will keep the vigil here."

"We won't be long," Hugh promised them. "If this weather holds, we might even build a beach fire for tea afterwards."

Liz groaned. "Don't mention food. I won't recover for hours as it is."

"You'll feel differently when we get back," he said. "The salt air will make a new woman of you."

Liz leaned back on an elbow. "I'd settle for a slimmer one. Have a good time."

Mike delayed a minute to give Carolyn some unsolicited advice. "See that you follow the doctor's orders and for God's sake, don't start any rock-climbing expeditions."

Liz saw the red of battle surge into Caro's cheeks and cut in before she could flare back. "I'll watch her, Mike. Don't worry about us ... sleeping and breathing deeply are the only two things on the agenda."

A muscle jerked along his tight jaw as he stared down at Carolyn's mutinous face. Then he sighed audibly before turning and striding down the beach after Hugh.

"Damn that man!" Carolyn exploded. "I hired him as a driver and he's tried to run my life ever since. No wonder he prefers European women. They're used to letting a man have his way. Only on the surface, of course," she amended. "Probably Gina bosses him around like crazy and he doesn't even know it."

"Could be." Liz brushed sand from her cheek and stretched out more comfortably on a blanket. "Why don't you ask him?"

"Because I haven't the slightest interest in his personal life." She stared after the men's dwindling figures and added paradoxically, "I wonder how long they'll be gone?"

"Who knows? Long enough for me to take a nap," Liz told her easily. "Amazing how the wind has died. It's almost balmy in the shelter of the cliff, isn't it?"

Carolyn nodded without interest.

"Why don't you rest for a while?" Liz urged. "You still look a trifle green around the edges."

"I don't *feel* green," Carolyn said stubbornly, and then relented. "All right ... I'm sorry. I don't know why I let that man make me so mad." She unfolded another blanket and stretched out on it. "It's a pity he can't take a few lessons from Hugh."

Liz opened one eye. "What kind of lessons?"

"Not the kind you're dreaming about. Liz, you have a terrible mind."

The eye closed. "Stop letting your imagination gallop. Frankly, I think both of them are charming. It's a pity I'm not twenty years younger to give you some competition."

Carolyn merely snorted and refused to respond to her teasing. Instead she let her glance wander down to the waterline, where the waves were advancing in their neat, measured layers. How quiet it was! The gentle sound of the surf hung in the tranquil afternoon air. Not even a sea bird wheeled overhead. Strange that there weren't some clinging to the rock ribs above them. She turned her head slowly and surveyed the dull gray overhang. The switchback path looked like erratic sewing machine stitching up the middle of the rough stone surface. Her gaze stopped by the spot where the rock slide had crashed over her, but there wasn't a single reminder left. If she had been knocked unconscious and her body had fallen down the jagged rock face . . . there wouldn't have been a reminder, either. A shudder coursed through her. When it came to human beings against the natural elements in Wales, nature would triumph every time.

She shaded her eyes and searched the top of the cliff. Impossible to see a sign of life anywhere. But the day before . . .

Her eyes narrowed as her thoughts raced on. The man in the fishing boat could have been looking at someone else with those binoculars. There could have been someone on that cliff above her. Only then, Mike would have seen him.

She moved restlessly, trying to find a more comfortable position on the hard sand beneath her. There was no point in trying to be a Monday morning quarterback. Anyone with imagination could think of a dozen logical explanations for that fishing boat being there and not one need have any sinister significance.

Her head went down on the blanket in sudden surrender. Just because she'd had an unpleasant experience, there was no need to have a trauma over it. She'd follow Liz's example and relax. After eating all that lunch, it was hard to do anything else.

When the sound of the motor first occurred, it fitted into the sequence of a half-waking dream and Carolyn didn't bother to open her eyes. It was only after the noise took on a staccato quality of a missing engine that she sat up abruptly and gazed wildly out to sea.

There was nothing on the water and, once again, the silence was unbroken.

She started to lie back down, convinced that it had all been a vivid dream, when the noise of the engine came again. It spluttered feebly at first and then gained momentum into a steady roar.

Carolyn frowned and stood up—wide awake now and trying to locate the source. The boat must be behind the fiordlike finger of rock to the north. It had to be! She listened carefully, her head cocked to one side. Surely it sounded the same as the fishing boat had yesterday.

If she could only see it! Once she had confirmed it was definitely the same boat, she could ask Hugh or Reese why it was cruising the castle waters on successive days.

She glanced down at Liz's motionless figure.

Evidently the noise hadn't disturbed her afternoon nap. It seemed a shame to waken her over vague suspicions. She was still hesitating when the pitch of sound changed. The boat owner must have throttled back and accelerated. At that rate, he'd be out of sight up the coast in short order.

Almost automatically, Carolyn started running toward the long stone promontory to catch a glimpse of him before he disappeared. As she hurried along the gravel beach near the water's edge, she thought what a good thing it was that she'd changed clothes for their picnic. At least tennis shoes and slacks were the ideal costume for clambering up rocks.

She was breathing hard when she finally reached the rock jetty, and the sound of the boat motor was getting fainter every minute. If she didn't get to the top of the rock ridge in short order, the boat would be gone entirely.

From ground level, the difficulties in climbing the ridge became apparent immediately. While the rocky rib wasn't particularly high, the sides were dreadfully sheer. Without help or the proper climbing gear, she wouldn't have a chance of scaling them. The access eased as the ridge protruded into the water but that meant she would need a boat as well.

"Which I don't have," she muttered to herself. "Damn! Now I know why they scheduled the practice assaults for Mt. Everest here in Wales."

Even as she stood there—an arrested study in

frustration—the sound of the motor faded beyond hearing. Belatedly she decided it would have been far better to climb the cliff path rather than come down the beach. Even halfway up the hillside, she would have been able to see over the rock spine. So much for feminine logic!

She kicked at a pebble on the beach and watched it arc toward the water. There was nothing left but to trudge back and tell Liz of her failure.

She wandered higher up the beach to softer sand and then paused once again. As long as she was in the area, she might as well look into the sea cave at the base of the cliff. It wasn't necessary to wait for Hugh to accompany her on such a simple sightseeing expedition. After taking a precautionary look over her shoulder to check the tide level, she strolled up to the tremendous opening. This was certainly not the time to play the idiot and have to wade through water to get out. Even the thought of Mike's reaction to that occurrence made her shudder.

Fortunately there seemed to be plenty of time, but she quickened her pace to avoid taking any chances. This way, she'd have a "quick in and then quick out" like a Rothschild in the stock market before she could get in trouble.

A lofty arch marked the opening to the sea cave with damp markings at either side showing where the waves poured through at high tide. The clusters of boulders at the front looked as if a giant hand had thrust them aside so that the sea could find its way.

Cautiously Carolyn made her way past them into the cavity and stood for a moment staring up at the vaulted ceiling. She was scarcely able to believe that the room around her had been carved by the abrasive action of the sea. It was fully thirty feet high and probably forty feet in depth. At one side, the rock wall formed a natural pathway which disappeared into the shadows at the back.

Hugh had explained earlier that the Welsh caves were caused by cracks along the shore hundreds of thousands of years ago. Apparently the cracks came about after movement of the earth's crust and marine action, through the years, enlarged the cracks with a scouring process to form the sea caves themselves. The sand and gravel carried by the water did the actual work, leaving the hollowed-out interior behind them.

"There's a splendid cave in the Scottish Hebrides," he had gone on to explain. "Mendelssohn was so taken with its beauty that he named his famous overture after it. Even the caves here in Wales have had a tremendous effect on our local folklore. Surely you've heard the legend of the sleeping Arthur?"

The three of them had shaken their heads, too intrigued to answer.

"It's an excellent story," Hugh told them, "and I'm firmly convinced that all the old-time inhabitants really believe it. King Arthur is reputed to be sleeping in one of our caves—surrounded by all his men from the Island of the Mighty. Many years ago, a man of west Wales who was the seventh son of a seventh son discovered the sleeping force."

"Why the seventh son of a seventh son?" Liz asked.

"Because only one of those has the necessary blending of man and the fairies to be granted inner sight," Hugh replied promptly. "This young man stumbled upon Arthur's forces when he discovered a cave and was told they were waiting there for an invasion by the enemies of Cymru. At that time, the soldiers will ride out with Arthur at their head and drive their foes into the sea. Wales will be kept safe as long as the earth endures." Hugh lowered his voice dramatically. "Any Welshman knows that he must not disturb the sleeping army in the cave until the final day of danger or his own life will be imperiled. That's why we treat our caves with the greatest respect."

Those words came back to Carolyn as she stood on the threshold of the sea cavern and she shivered suddenly, despite herself.

"Idiot!" she said, giving herself a mental prod.

There were no sleeping soldiers lining the walls—only rocks stained in shades of green and pink by their mineral deposits. Seaweed tossed carelessly alongside in shallow water tidal pools

163

left its dark green mark. The sound of dripping water came down the wall by her side. Probably a spring on the hillside above had found its outlet through the rock. As the minutes went by and she moved carefully around the rugged interior, the spell wrought by Hugh's story wore off.

It took a flash of white near the ceiling to make her recall it abruptly. Then she laughed aloud ... although her eyes stayed carefully glued to the spot. There was nothing supernatural about that movement. If her ears were right, she had discovered the hiding place of Mrs. Reese's cat.

There was another flicker of movement up above and once again the faint mewing.

"Kitty ... kitty," Carolyn coaxed. "Come down ... nice kitty."

The only response was a disdainful wave of the tail as the young cat remained stubbornly on his rocky perch.

"Darn!" Carolyn frowned in concentration and then her brow cleared. There was a magic phrase for the gray tomcat who lived in Liz's apartment which was guaranteed to bring him running from the next block.

She tried it out. "Would you like to eat, kitty?"

The white ball remained uncooperatively still. No wonder, Carolyn decided belatedly. Undoubtedly Mrs. Reese spoke to her cat in Welsh. She was caught behind the language barrier once again! "Sorry, kitty," she said with amusement, "I forgot to bring my phrase book along."

This time there was an audible meow.

"I know," Caro was sympathetic. "This communication gap is terrible." She held out an entreating hand. "If you'd just come down, I could give you some fine fish paste sandwiches." Her voice lowered confidentially. "Frankly, I'd be delighted if you'd polish them off ... otherwise they'll be offered again at tea." She stood quietly, but the cat didn't budge.

Carolyn gave an exasperated sigh. It would be nice to take the stubborn cat back with her. If she just went back to their picnic spot and waited for Hugh to return, the cat would probably be gone by the time they got back to the cave.

She explored the rough access to the upper regions of the cavern with her eyes. It shouldn't be too difficult to get up there and rescue the cat herself. Those outcroppings made easy stepping-stones near the bottom and there were plenty of handholds further along the wall. With rubber-soled shoes, she should be able to manage.

She directed another quick glance at the motionless cat and instructed him softly. "Now ... stay there and behave yourself until I come up and rescue you." Her eyes narrowed thoughtfully. "Although I'm not sure you really need rescuing. I think you're just too darned stubborn to come down."

As if to confirm this statement, the cat calmly started to wash a front paw.

Carolyn shook her head hopelessly and moved

over to the beginning of the rough path. "I'll remember that," she told her captive audience. "Fish paste may be too good for you, after all."

After that, she abandoned conversation and concentrated on finding the easiest way up. At first, there was no difficulty. From the looks of it, the route had been used many times before. Probably by sightseers and kids, she decided, scrambling carefully around a jagged rock. Her thoughts went back to Hugh's story of coastal smuggling. This was the kind of cave those men could have used. It was certainly big enough. She looked down again to gauge the size of the entrance. At high tide, a small boat could be brought completely inside and hidden from view. Not her fishing boat, though, she concluded. It was too large—so she could eliminate it on that score.

What a fool she was to even think about such things! Smuggling hadn't been practiced around here in years. This was Wales ... not some Iron Curtain country which was short on consumer goods. Yesterday's experience must have addled her thinking more than she realized. Mike was probably right with his warning.

Mike! Good lord, he had specifically warned her against doing exactly what she *was* doing at the moment. He'd explode like a rocket if he ever found out. It didn't matter that he had no logical reason for his dogmatic attitude or that his doses of advice were about as welcome as sulphur and molasses. The fact remained that it would be considerably more peaceful for all concerned if she were back and suitably at rest when he returned.

She turned around and was starting to retrace her steps when the half-grown cat protested again.

"Meow-rr!" The translation came out "I want food" in any language. To emphasize the point, he got up and stood poised on the edge of his perch.

"Don't fall off, for pete's sake," Caro muttered as she turned back toward him. She'd have to get the darned cat whatever Mike thought! After all, she was old enough to make a simple decision for herself and this little climb wasn't going to bother anyone. Her labored breathing soon refuted some of her argument, but she kept doggedly on.

The cat was much nearer now and shrank back nervously as she approached.

"Don't worry, kitty . . . I won't hurt you. Just take it easy until I can find a place here for my foot. . . ." Her shoe slid up and down the rock to her left, fumbling for a toehold. No luck.

Carolyn screwed up her face in concentration. There must be a way to get up there! She dislodged a shower of stones with her movements and heard them slither down to the cavern floor. Her eyes closed just for an instant . . . remembering . . . fearing. Then they flashed open again. There was no reason to be so skittish. Even if she fell here, she'd merely scrape some skin. It wasn't like yesterday.

She pushed herself along on her elbows and tried for a new foothold further to the left. There! Her toe slid in. She'd found one! Putting her weight on it, she started to move across the rock and reach for the cat. Suddenly her foot lurched down into a crevass between two vertical slabs . . . lurched down and stuck.

"Ouch!" Carolyn shifted her handholds and tried to pull her leg upward. My God . . . she couldn't budge it! Frantically then, she yanked her foot and stopped immediately as a twinge of pain shot up her instep. If she kept that up, she'd really be in trouble.

"Meow-rr," the cat said again from his vantage point three feet above.

"Skip the conversation," Carolyn informed it, "unless you know some way to pry me out of here."

There was no answer to that. The cat's cold stare indicated, more plainly than words, that human beings were good for supplying saucers of chopped liver and very little else.

"Well, if you won't help. . . ." Carolyn tried twisting her foot from another angle and failed again. There was no hope for it, she decided disconsolately. What she really needed was a derrick. And derricks were in short supply.

"Damn!" she said.

The cat curled his lip at such weakness and started to lick the other paw.

"You know it's all your fault!"

The pink cat tongue didn't miss a lick at that pronouncement either and Carolyn fell silent, wondering if she'd have any better luck convincing Michael.

She rested her hip against a niche in the rock behind her and tried to make herself comfortable while waiting for the rescue squad. Once Hugh and Michael discovered her absence, it shouldn't take long for them to narrow the list of trouble spots. She wanted to see the face of her watch and check the time but found that the gloom of the rock overhang made it impossible. At least she could be thankful that she was in no danger from the incoming tide. From the watermarks on the cave walls, she was easily four or five feet above the reach of high water . . . unless there was some freak tidal action.

A cold ripple of air brushed past her shoulders and she wrapped her arms over her breast for extra warmth. If she'd known she was going to spend the afternoon in a cave, she certainly would have worn something heavier than a poplin jacket over her cotton shirt.

Time passed so slowly that it seemed each minute was reluctant to give way to the next. Even the little white cat gave up eventually and settled to an afternoon nap. Carolyn surveyed its tight, ball-like figure and wished she could curl up in the same way.

The temperature in the vaulted space felt as if it had dropped alarmingly and she was starting to wonder if icicles formed at night when she finally heard the sound of footsteps on the gravel beach. It was a determined stride which caused her to stifle her first impulse to cry out. Instead she shrank back with her heart pounding and her cheeks as pale as the gray stone beside her. When Mike's tall figure moved into the cave opening all she could see was a block of shadow, but there was no mistaking that stern voice.

"Carolyn?" It wasn't actually a query . . . just a cold, controlled word. "Where are you this time?"

She swallowed once before saying meekly, "Up here."

He reacted like a wild animal getting a troublesome scent. There was instant arrested movement, then an intent searching gaze which didn't take long. He started climbing immediately once he caught sight of her cowering figure. Unfortunately the movement didn't interfere with his powers of speech.

"Why in the hell are you hanging around up there?"

She had trouble deciding whether to laugh or cry. "Hanging around is certainly an apt way of putting it."

He was beside her then—having made child's

play of the climb. "What's happened? Are you hurt?"

"Not really. It's my foot ... the left one. Somehow I managed to wedge it in a crack."

He pushed past her and ran gentle fingers along her leg as far down as he could reach. "Any pain?"

"No. I simply can't get enough leverage in this position to pull it out."

His glance swept over her comprehensively. "I think I can supply that if I can hoist you up and sideways at the same time." He started to rearrange his position accordingly. "Now—put your arms around my neck." He gave her an exasperated look. "Tight, for God's sake ... so you can hang on."

She obliged wordlessly. If her death grip had any emotional effect on him, he certainly hid it successfully, she decided.

He merely concentrated on the crack where her foot disappeared and said tersely, "Try wriggling your shoe when I lift you. Sing out if it hurts."

"Why? I have to get out."

"Don't be a nitwit. If I can't pry you out this way, I'll go get a chisel and start on the rock."

She gave an audible gulp. "I didn't think ..."

"Do you ever?" He didn't wait for an answer but started lifting her gently. "Here we go ... try all the angles. Any luck?"

"I don't think so. . . ." She bit down on her lip as her shin scraped against a sharp piece of rock. Then she gasped, "Oh yes! Keep pulling, Mike. My shoe was stuck but it's giving way . . . there!" She surged upward like a cork from a bottle and he staggered, trying to keep his balance.

"Okay?" he asked finally as the two of them clung together on the narrow ledge.

She nodded but said ruefully, "I've lost my shoe."

"Hell's fire . . . who cares about that. Try using your foot."

"I will . . . if you'll put me down far enough to touch the ground."

"Oh." For the first time, he sounded non-plussed himself. She was lowered immediately although he kept a careful supporting arm around her shoulders. "How is it?"

Gingerly, she let her weight rest on her left side. Looking up, she said, "Fine, I think. Right now there are a million prickles."

"That's the circulation returning. Once I get you down to the beach, I'll massage it." He gave another quick look around. "Come on—this seems the easiest way."

"But my shoe . . ."

"Leave it. I'll buy you a new pair. Hang on to me as we go down."

She was stung by his diffident manner. "I'll buy my own pair," she retorted hotly.

There was no answer. He obviously couldn't

care less, she decided, so there was no reason for her to be depressed. Certainly it was no way to feel after just being rescued. She glanced sideways at him. If he'd only display a token amount of interest it would be reassuring. Hugh wouldn't treat a woman in such cavalier fashion. Hugh would . . .

She spoke her thoughts aloud. "Where *is* Hugh?"

"Probably on the way," he replied laconically. "He was going to check with Liz to see if you'd gone up to the castle. Once he finds you're not there, he'll be back."

"How did you know where to look?"

"I just picked the most unlikely, hard-to-get-at, dangerous, and uncomfortable spot that a woman like you would make for. . . ."

"And?" They were down to beach level now and she dropped his supporting arm as if it were red hot.

"There you were. Sit down on that rock and let me rub your leg."

"I don't want you to. . . ."

"I said, sit down!"

She sat. "Don't roar at me like that," she said finally.

He crouched in front of her and started kneading the muscles of her leg. "You're right . . . it takes more than roaring."

"What does?"

"Anything to make you act like a sensible human being . . . for a change." His fingers bit into her calf. "What the devil were you doing in here in the first place?"

She was too tired to fight. "Trying to rescue Mrs. Reese's cat."

If she expected sympathy, she'd guessed wrong. He looked up, frowning. "For pete's sake, why?"

"He was stuck on a ledge up there."

Mike lowered his head again. "I see. Where is he now?"

"I forgot to look. Her gaze went back to the rocks above them. "Why . . . he's gone!"

"Of course he is." Mike gave a final slap to her shin and stood up. "Don't you know anything about cats? He was probably in a lot better fix than you were. Even if he wasn't . . . why didn't you come back for help?"

"I thought he might disappear."

"Then he wouldn't have been stuck," he said with maddening logic.

She put her hands up to her temples. "Oh, stop rubbing it in. I know I acted stupidly. I make a habit of it when you're around."

He shoved his hands in his pockets, absently jingling some coins. "Now you *are* being ridiculous. Sit there and rest for a minute so you can get back up the beach."

"I wish you'd stop giving me orders."

"And I wish to God you'd take a few of them. Otherwise you'll go back across the Atlantic on a stretcher."

"I'm perfectly capable of running my own life." Her chin jutted as stubbornly as his. "You might remember that I didn't hire a bodyguard—merely a driver." Even as she spoke, she wondered why she was goading him. Why she was taking such a perverse delight in his irritated reaction to her taunts—watching his eyes become flintlike as they returned her defiant stare.

"So I'm a hired hand," he replied softly, taking a purposeful step forward. His easy manners had completely disappeared and he looked as dangerous as a barracuda circling his prey. "Thanks for reminding me of my place."

Carolyn shrugged, a little frightened at his response. "Now who's getting carried away," she said, trying to keep her voice steady. "All I'm trying to get across is that I'm quite capable of making decisions—I've been doing it right along. You can save your advice for your girlfriend back home."

"Any other words of wisdom?"

She should have taken heed from the way he chipped out those words—as if each one were a separate sliver of ice. Instead she raised her chin still higher and said, "That's all except I hope you're keeping an account of your time and expenses for this trip."

"Oh, I am." His voice showed cold amusement now. "Of course, I charge extra for pulling females off ledges. . . ."

"There you go again," she replied, stung by

the sarcasm. "If I don't give way to your orders, you start reading the riot act—and that wasn't in our agreement. Just skip the editorial opinions, Mr. Evans, and hand in your time sheet when we're ready to leave."

"Very well. If that's the way you feel, Miss Drummond." He put as much stress on the formal title as she had. "You can start paying on account now." He reached out and pulled her close against him before she was aware what was happening. "I don't think we ever discussed the amount of my day rate. . . ." One strong hand clamped her against his chest and he grabbed a fistful of her hair with the other.

"What are you doing?" Her voice rose in a wail.

"Putting in part of my expense account. Next time, get your terms in writing."

"There won't *be* a next time. . . ."

"Then I'd better make the most of this, hadn't I?" Deliberately, ruthlessly, his lips came down to cover hers.

After the first ten seconds, Carolyn forgot to struggle. After the first thirty seconds, Mike's grip shifted to let her willing arms go around his neck.

When that long kiss ended, both of them surfaced unsteadily for the return to reality. They clung together, breathing hard. Mike stared down at her and shook his head as if to clear it.

176

"Mike ... darling ..." Her tremulous whisper trailed off as his eyes darkened.

Then he'd pulled her pliant figure back against the hard length of him and was kissing her in a way that made her senses reel.

She pushed away from him finally before she lost every smidgin of willpower. His clasp loosened reluctantly.

"Why did you kiss me like that?" she managed eventually, still clinging to the front of his jacket.

There was a stifled chuckle. "Overtime duty," he replied solemnly. "I charge double for weekends. Wait until we work up to holiday pay."

Carolyn made a desperate attempt to regain her senses. What in the world was the matter with her! Just because a man kissed her twice. No ... that last one was more than a kiss. Call it an earthquake and a volcanic eruption rolled into one! She still felt as if she were in the after-shock. Dazedly she looked up at him. It was impossible to ask if he felt that way too.

Undoubtedly he'd kissed hundreds of women just as expertly. Probably it was the regular bill of fare for Gina. Carolyn suddenly pushed away from him with arms that had regained their strength. The man could find his holiday amusement elsewhere!

"I'm sorry about your extra hours," she managed stiffly, "but playtime's over. Next time I hire temporary help, I'll ask for references first." She turned and stumbled toward the entrance to the cave. If she could have found a deep hole to crawl into, it would have been even better. Thank goodness, he didn't know that the last few minutes had been far more painful than having her ankle caught in the rocks.

It was no use trying to pretend that she had been immune to his lovemaking. Her whole-hearted response could have left him in no doubt as to her feelings. He was probably chuckling about it even now.

Hugh's tall figure silhouetted at the cave entrance provided a welcome diversion.

"Carolyn ... is that you?" He called uncertainly.

"Yes, I'm here. Oh Hugh, I'm so glad you've come!"

There was no disguising the welcome in her voice and Hugh simply opened his arms. She flew into them and buried her head against his chest.

"Hugh ... I never thought I'd be so happy to see anybody."

He was patently astounded but not about to question his good fortune. His arms tightened and he bent his head to kiss her softly. "Carolyn, my dear ... why, you're crying!" His finger brushed her damp cheek. "Not to worry, love. You're safe now." He turned her toward the beach, keeping a protective arm around her shoulders. "I thought Mike was going to inspect that cave or I would have been along before this. Liz is terribly worried about you, so we'd best go along and reassure her. You *are* all right, aren't you?"

"Perfectly." Resolutely Carolyn kept her gaze ahead of them. There was to be no looking back ... ever.

"That's the girl!" His arm tightened affectionately. "Welsh sea caves are spooky places but I always say there's no real danger in them."

Carolyn stumbled slightly and then regained her stride.

She didn't quarrel with his reasoning, but this time she could have told him he'd reached the wrong conclusion.

Chapter Eight

When Liz ran her to earth a half-hour later, Carolyn was propped up on her bed leafing disconsolately through a pamphlet put out by the Wales Tourist Board.

"So here you are," Liz said in some relief. "We all thought you were coming down for the cocktail hour. Why didn't you? It's warmer down there if nothing else. You *are* feeling all right, aren't you?"

"Of course. I thought Hugh told you. He hovered over me like an anxious parent all the way back."

"Was that bad?" Liz perched on the side of the bed and reached over to study the title of Carolyn's pamphlet. *"South Wales—Gwent between Usk and Wye,"* she read carefully. "It sounds like something on a sandwich menu. Why in the world are you reading that?"

Carolyn tossed the booklet onto a bed table. "Because there wasn't anything else around except a book on *Disasters at Sea* ... and I didn't feel like making conversation downstairs."

"You aren't the only one," Liz said, leaning back against the bed post. "Mike just came in a few minutes ago. He was looking as gloomy as a giraffe with a sore throat and darned if he didn't ask Hugh about road conditions in north Wales. Did he say anything to you about moving on?"

"I don't think he mentioned it," Carolyn said carefully.

"Then you *did* see him in the cave?"

Carolyn fixed her with a baleful stare. "Why don't you stop being subtle and just ask what you want to know."

Liz was undeterred. "All right. What happened between the two of you this afternoon?"

"Nothing spectacular," Carolyn said evasively. "We agreed to disagree again." That part, at least, was true.

"Honestly—you're both hopeless."

"I'd be the first to agree with you. Are we changing for dinner tonight?"

"You might put on a skirt for the sake of Reese's old-world sensibilities."

"I'd already planned on that." Caro pushed off the bed and went over to survey her meager collection of dresses in the wardrobe. "What's on the agenda after dinner?"

"Hugh wants to drive over to Tenby, but I'll have to stay around until my call comes through."

Carolyn glanced back at her. "What call?"

"Didn't I tell you? I *am* losing my mind these days." Liz tapped her temple significantly. "Henry called earlier while we were down on the beach. Reese says the call has been placed again for tonight. He very carefully wrote down all the details and gave them to me." She fished a memo from the pocket of her skirt and held it out.

Carolyn took it and read the cramped writing. "I wonder what old Henry has on his mind?"

"You know Henry," Liz said with resignation. "He's either tired of waiting for our report or he's found a new weekend villa on the Yugoslavian coast somewhere. I wish he'd find a new hobby to occupy his mind." She was threading her fingers along the edge of the tasseled bedspread. "Do you suppose he'd go for tropical fish?" There was no reply and she glanced up to see Carolyn's stricken face. "Sweetie—what is it?"

Carolyn ignored that. "Liz—where did you get this note?"

"I *told* you. Reese gave it to me. What's wrong with that? Obviously he wanted to get Henry's message straight."

"I don't mean Henry's message," Carolyn interrupted. "This paper—it's just like the other one."

183

"What other one?" Liz stood up and put a solicitous hand on Carolyn's forehead. "Maybe you're running a temperature after the excitement yesterday."

The other pushed her gently back on the bed. "Don't be silly, Liz. Now—sit there and listen. This paper ..." she emphasized, "is from Wellington Foods."

"What's wrong with that? Probably Reese found an old scrap of paper by the telephone and used it for his message."

"Don't you remember? It was a piece of paper just like this when I tangled with the van in Chepstow. That was an invoice for cheese and this one's blank, but the printed heading is identical. It's a strange coincidence ... don't you think?"

"I don't know." Liz frowned fiercely. "Maybe you're making too much of it. It could be like finding a pack of book matches with advertising printed on the cover at home. They're all over the place. Besides," she pointed out, "you don't know for sure that your piece of paper had anything to do with that truck hitting you."

Carolyn sagged onto the bed beside her. "I know. I wish you'd stop being logical. Actually I've thought of all those things myself."

"Would it do any good to ask Reese?" Liz put in hopefully.

Carolyn shook her head. "I doubt it. He's given me that polite blank look every time I've asked a question so far. Hugh's the only one who can get anything out of him."

"Well, then . . . ask Hugh."

"How can I?" Carol made a helpless gesture. "After making that fuss about hearing noises in my room the other night. Can't you just see his expression if I ask why Reese has a piece of paper from a food company in the kitchen. He'll think I'm . . ." she searched for the right expression.

"Crackers is the word they use over here," Liz said dryly. "Stark, raving crackers."

Carolyn sighed. "That's it, then. The worst part is—I'm not sure myself. You're not convinced either and you're supposed to be on my side."

"I know. Look, Caro—the logical person to ask about this is Michael. You must realize that."

"I don't see why. . . ." the younger woman's voice trailed off as she intercepted Liz's look of disdain. Finally she said flatly, "I can't."

"Don't be silly. Of course you can!" Liz stood up. "I'll go tell him to come up here since this doesn't come under the heading of drawing room conversation." She looked at her watch. "Besides, it's about time for Henry's call to come through. I should be waiting for it this time."

"Give Henry my best. . . ."

"I will." Liz paused on her way to the door. "For heaven's sake, put some lipstick on."

Carolyn's expression turned stubborn. "Why? I'm not trying to impress anyone." After that session in the cave, it would be a wonder if Mike came near—even at Liz's bidding.

"Who's talking about impressing anyone? There's no reason for you to go around looking pale like the heroine in a Victorian novel." Liz pulled open the door. "I'll have Mike up here in five minutes." The door closed behind her with a soft thud.

Stung by her words, Carolyn pulled the red knit off a hanger and slipped into it without further delay. She had just finished combing her hair and applying a bright lipstick when a knock sounded from the hall.

Hastily dropping the lipstick back in her purse, she hurried over to open the door.

Michael stood there. "Liz said you wanted to talk to me." His voice was as expressionless as his face.

Carolyn felt a wave of despair wash over her. Whatever she had been hoping when she saw him again, it wasn't confrontation by a cold-voiced stranger who had come only because of Liz's command.

"I need some advice ... won't you come in." She stepped aside politely and closed the door behind him.

"Thanks."

He moved over to the fireplace and leaned against the mantel. Carolyn noted idly that his gray sports coat and slacks blended with the muted colors of the tapestry behind him.

Evidently he had been rehearsing his next words for they came out immediately. "I want to apologize for my remarks ... and for what happened down in the cave. I didn't mean to offend you." He was concentrating on Poppa Bear's recumbent form next to the hearth as if willing him to rise from his prone position and act as intermediary.

"It was partly my fault," Caro acknowledged.

Mike's shrug indicated he didn't really care. "That's immaterial. There was no need for me to lose my temper and take it out on you."

She could have told him then that the episode in the cave wasn't half as heartbreaking as this polite withdrawal. If she had remembered that the Sweetheart Spoon was destined for Gina all along, she could have avoided some misery. Obviously Mike had merely been carried away for the moment and had belatedly come to his senses. And since he was a decent, civilized man, he naturally felt badly about straying from the beaten path. The fact that she'd discovered she was in love with him an hour ago didn't matter.

Even the thought of it made her wince.

"I feel like a damned fool," he said, catching the tail end of her fleeting expression. "Frankly, I haven't acted like that in years. At least Hugh didn't appear at the crucial moment and make things worse."

"Hugh?"

"He didn't catch on, did he? I don't think he

187

saw me but if you want me to go and explain it was all a mistake. . . ."

She shook her head helplessly. "Good heavens, no!"

"I didn't think you did." He shoved his hands deep in his pockets. "You could do worse than Hugh. He's a nice fellow when you get to know him."

"Are you supplying references now?" There was a bitter undertone to her words. It was bad enough to be shunted aside for another woman without his deciding her future at the same time.

"Don't get het up. I was just saying that . . ."

"I know what you're saying," she interrupted, "and I wish you'd keep your good wishes until they're needed."

A wave of red surged up under his cheekbones. "Falling in love hasn't improved that temper of yours one bit!"

"You're a fine one to talk." It was a relief to let fly in her misery. "Coming in here and lecturing like some marriage counselor. Hugh and I are managing very well without your help. Why don't you go and pack or finish whatever you were doing."

"I'll be glad to," he said tersely, moving toward the door. "I don't know why I was so damned foolish as to listen to Liz. . . ." He stopped abruptly and turned to give her a sheepish look. "What in the devil *did* I come up here for?"

She broke out in unwilling laughter and sank

down on the low chest at the end of the bed. "I'd forgotten, too. Mike, I'm as big a fool as you are. Come back here and sit down." She patted the end of the chest. "Let's declare a truce for five minutes at least."

"I'd like that," he admitted, sitting down beside her. He picked up her hand and gave it a comforting squeeze. "What do you say we forget the last five minutes and start over instead."

"I'd like that," she mimicked gently, letting her hand stay in his grasp. "Now listen ... and then tell me if I'm losing my mind." Briefly she explained finding the Wellington Foods heading on Reese's memo. "I don't know whether to confront Reese with it or forget the whole thing," she said finally. "What do you think?"

He frowned and didn't answer for a minute. "Damned if I know," he said then. "Frankly I'd rather you stayed out of it." He saw the gleam in her eyes and added, "You asked for that advice, remember?"

"I suppose so," she admitted, wishing she could yield to her impulse and rest her head against his tweed-clad shoulder. "But if I don't inquire—who could? I don't want to bring Hugh into this. He has enough problems of his own right now."

"Now you're being stupid again," he said gently, "and you're doing Hugh an injustice. Any man would want to protect his girl when she was in trouble. Besides, he's the only one who can get a straight story from Reese. I'll ask Hugh about it . . . if you want me to," he added uncertainly.

"Let's wait until Liz talks to Henry, at least. If he still plans on buying the castle, things should be easier."

Mike shrugged. "Whatever you say . . . though I can't see where it makes any difference. If Hugh loves you—then he loves you whether this blasted castle is sold or not. Don't tell me he's laying down conditions?"

"I'd rather not discuss it," Carolyn said shakily.

"Well, it's nice to know where I stand. Believe it or not, I *am* interested."

"I know, Mike, but I simply can't explain." She let her hand rest on his sleeve for a moment and then stood up to put a safer distance between them.

His imagination had leaped so far that it was impossible to set him straight without an embarrassing declaration on her part, so it was best to let his assumption ride. Once they left Lyonsgate, their paths wouldn't meet again. She would see to that—for her own protection.

He stood as well, taking the memo from her and putting it in his jacket pocket. "I'll go down now and see what Hugh thinks. . . ." His words broke off as a knock came at the door.

"May I join your conclave?" Liz asked, poking her head around the jamb. "I've just finished talking to Henry." She shut the door behind her and came over to perch on the arm of a chair.

"What's new?" Carolyn asked.

Liz shook her head. "Wales is out and western Florida is in. He's just bought a showplace on Sanibel Island. Somebody talked him into collecting shells for a hobby and he wants to spend all his spare time on the beach there."

Carolyn made a grimace of frustration. "Wouldn't you know! Now what do we tell Hugh?"

"The truth, of course," Liz answered. "He won't throw us out tonight."

"I didn't mean that. It's just that he wanted to sell this place so badly."

"This isn't the end of everything," Mike put in. "There'll be other chances."

Liz pulled on her ear lobe. "I'll bet they're few and far between, though. Henry wants me to write a generous check for any inconvenience we've caused."

"Liz—you wouldn't!" Carolyn said spiritedly. "Hugh would hate that."

"I know. Even though he could probably use the money. Don't worry, sweetie. I'll try to think of something more diplomatic. Unfortunately there isn't an easy way for me to say that our Henry doesn't want to buy the old homestead." She opened her purse and absently rooted for her cigarettes. Suddenly she paused and held up a piece of paper. "There was one other thing ... I meant to show you this." She handed the scrap over to Mike. "It's more of the same."

"You mean another memo from Wellington

Foods?" Carolyn asked as she went to peer over his shoulder.

"We're practically knee-deep in them," Liz confirmed. "I should have remembered it before."

"This one was supplied by Mrs. Reese?" Mike asked.

She nodded. "It has that recipe on it that I wanted. I don't know where she found the piece of paper."

"Maybe they bought a boxful at the local thrift shop," Caro said.

"I doubt that." Mike turned to Liz. "When are you going to tell Hugh about the real estate deal falling through?"

She stood up, looking slightly baffled. "Right away, I suppose. I might as well get it over with. Why?"

He opened the door for her. "Because I want to ask him about this paper, but I don't want to interrupt your conference."

She looked at her watch. "Give me fifteen minutes."

"Take your time. I have some packing to do first. Later on, I want to drive into Tenby on business. Why don't we all have dinner there? A look at the bright lights might cheer Hugh." His glance flickered across the room. "What do you think, Carolyn?"

"It sounds fine—except that Mrs. Reese has probably started dinner here."

"Then she can take it out of the oven or do whatever is necessary. Don't look so disapproving. I'm sure she'll be glad to get rid of us for the evening. Go lay the groundwork, Liz."

"I'll be glad to. A night out will do us all some good."

The night out didn't quite come up to Liz's hopes. The only hotel which would serve them dinner in the Welsh resort town looked as if it had been built during the reign of Henry VIII. Liz contended that this added a certain charm but didn't do much for the creature comforts. They ate their dinner in a drafty ballroom, sitting on rickety gilt chairs and listening to a dismal program of chamber music. The members of the string trio were overweight, middle-aged women wearing identically grim blue taffeta evening dresses.

After a particularly trying Mozart opus, Hugh said, "I understand now why the Beatles were given the Order of the British Empire for their outstanding services."

"It's a pity they weren't serving dinner in that pub with the good pianist," Mike agreed, sawing at a lamb cutlet. "Oh well, the headwaiter says these ladies switch to dance music a little later."

"The way that waiter of ours carries one fork at a time," Liz observed, "the trio will have gone home by the time we reach dessert."

"In that case, we'll leap out on the floor the

first time they play anything written in the twentieth century," Hugh promised.

When the next musical number turned out to be a frightening rendition of "Red Sails in the Sunset," the four of them were laughing so hard that they could scarcely stand on the dance floor. Mike gravitated to Liz and Hugh happily clasped Carolyn in his arms.

"This makes the entire evening worthwhile," he said, performing a commendable fox trot. "It was certainly decent of Mike to suggest a night out for all of us."

"Especially since he's hardly been with us long enough to eat his dinner," Carolyn said irritably. "I wonder who he's telephoning that's so important?" Actually she had a very good idea who he was telephoning and it didn't raise her morale in the least.

Michael's tendency to treat her like a none-too-bright younger sister on the drive to Tenby hadn't helped, either. Even her appearance in her best black wool with the elegant white satin collar and cuffs had done nothing more than make the man ask whether she'd be warm enough on the ride home. It didn't improve her disposition to acknowledge that he was right and she wouldn't be. After that, she had been ushered into the back seat with Hugh and promptly forgotten.

At least Hugh didn't leave her wondering.

"You look gorgeous," he was saying enthusiastically as he circled the floor—staying as far away from the string trio as possible. "Are you sure you haven't a million dollars?"

"Absolutely positive," she said, grinning up at him. "Would a sweepstake ticket help?"

"I'll take it into account." His clasp tightened around her waist. "In your case, I'm thinking of making an exception."

"You're so nice, Hugh." She let her head rest against his shoulder. "I'm terribly sorry that old Henry phoned with such bad news."

He pressed a soft kiss to her forehead. "Forget it. Actually I didn't expect anything else. If I had thousands of American dollars to spend, I certainly wouldn't buy a Welsh castle with a leaking roof. When I get a flat in Hong Kong, at least I won't have to worry about the rain driving in."

"Or if it does, you'll merely phone the manager and complain."

"Exactly." He twirled her around the far end of the dance floor. "Wonderful place, Hong Kong! You're sure it doesn't tempt you?"

"Of course it does! I'd spend my last penny on their wonderful clothes."

"If they all looked as good on you as this dress, I wouldn't mind," he assured her. "Carolyn, I'm serious."

She pulled back in his hold and looked up at him. "I'm beginning to believe you are." She shook her head. "Don't be, Hugh. This is our night to . . ."

" . . . paint the town!" He interrupted with a chuckle. "In this mausoleum with that terrible trio playing. . . ." He cocked his head to listen. "What *are* they playing? My God, it can't be!"

"It is," she assured him. " 'Tiptoe through the Tulips' sounds just the same on this side of the Atlantic. Now I know what the travel agents mean when they say Wales is out of this world."

"Shame on you. There are some places in this country that would put swinging London in the shadow. Ask Mike."

"Why Mike? Has he been in Wales before?" Her tone was sharper than she realized.

"Of course. Didn't he tell you?" He paused to avoid two dancers bent on a collision course. "Evans is a very common Welsh name. Just like Jones or Smith in the United States."

"I never gave it a thought." She glanced casually around the floor and finally located Mike holding an animated conversation with Liz as they danced. He danced very well, she decided, after a longer scrutiny.

"That's a strange story he was telling about the memo paper," Hugh was saying. "I asked Reese, of course, but the old fellow didn't know anything about it."

Naturally, thought Carolyn. Aloud, she asked, "Did he have any idea where it came from?"

"Not unless his nephew left it behind after a visit."

She frowned, trying to remember what else she

had heard about Reese's nephew. There was something about the young man driving around the village on his periodic visits.

The music came to a wavering conclusion. There was sporadic applause from the dancers and then the couples strolled back to their tables as the musicians claimed a rest break.

Mike was standing behind his chair at the edge of the ballroom floor. "Are you two ready to leave?" he asked.

"I guess so," Carolyn said. "Where's Liz?"

He gestured toward the lobby. "Picking up her wrap. She'll meet us on the front steps."

"I suppose we should be on our way," Hugh agreed. "We still have quite a drive. Too bad you missed your chance to dance with Carolyn, Mike."

"Uh-huh." It was a noncommittal grunt.

Carolyn decided he could have sounded more regretful for appearances' sake, if nothing else. As he started to help her down the lobby stairs, she deliberately edged closer to Hugh and accepted his assistance.

"I'll see about getting the car," Mike said tersely and strode on ahead.

"What's bothering him tonight?" Hugh wondered.

"Maybe he got the wrong answers on some of his phone calls," Carolyn said flippantly. "We'll never know."

"You're right about that. He plans to leave

197

early tomorrow morning." He rubbed the side of his jaw. "Do you think he could be persuaded to stay longer?"

"Ask Liz. The two of them get along like a house afire. If he's en route to a tennis tournament, though, we wouldn't stand a chance."

"It's not that . . . there's another week before Wimbledon. Apparently he's just had a change in plans."

"Or his lady friend changed her plans," she said cynically.

Hugh was unconvinced. "He didn't say anything about it. Are you sure?"

"I'm sure of the woman. She's a beautiful, red-headed Italian."

He whistled softly. "That's quite a combination."

"Maybe she has a friend," she said with a mocking look.

"My dear Carolyn . . . Mike can keep his gorgeous Italians. I'm partial to lovely blonde Americans with hazel eyes."

"That's when you're not partial to lovely Scottish girls named Sylvia," she chided. Nodding her thanks to the uniformed attendant who held the door for them, she stepped gingerly out onto the wide stone porch of the hotel. "I hope Mike hurries with the car before we freeze out here. Where do you suppose Liz is?"

"Coming from the lobby right now," he said, "and there's the car, so we'll have you warm in no time." He leered theatrically. "One of the many advantages of sitting in the back seat."

On the ride home, the occupants of the back seat had only one contact with the driver in the front seat and that was a ten-second query regarding their comfort. For the rest of the time, Carolyn was treated to a long, uninterrupted look at the back of Mike's head.

When they arrived at Lyonsgate, Mike abruptly decanted the three of them at the front entrance and drove around to the back of the castle to put the car away.

Hugh caught Carolyn's elbow as she would have followed Liz up to the front door. "Wait a bit. I thought we might go for a stroll."

"I'll have to get a coat first," she parried.

"Take my wrap," Liz offered, shrugging off a smart white wool stole and handing it over. "It should keep you warm."

"I could have managed that in another way," Hugh said, grinning. "As you undoubtedly remember, Mrs. Sheppard."

Liz chuckled. "Believe it or not, I'd almost forgotten."

"That I don't believe." He opened the door for her. "I won't keep Carolyn out long. Be sure and ring for Reese if you and Michael would like something hot to drink."

"I will, thank you. 'Night, Hugh."

"Good night, Liz." He turned back to Carolyn, now comfortably swathed in the stole. "Ready?"

She nodded. "Which way?"

"Let's go down by the chapel. You can have a moonlight view of the sea from the headland."

"Your invitation would be more convincing if there was a decent moon. That little sliver up there is hardly enough to count."

He urged her forward on the path. "Then I'll tell you about the moonlight in Burma. You wouldn't believe how romantic those tropical nights could be . . . moonlight shining on their temples. . . ."

She giggled.

"Now what?" He slowed his pace.

"It sounded like something from Tin Pan Alley. You know, 'Moon over Rangoon'. . . ."

She was given a gentle shake before he pulled her closer to his side. "Keep on like that and I'll understand why your American men prefer Italian women. Stop making jokes when I'm trying to get you in the proper mood."

"It's safer to make jokes," she said firmly. "What about Sylvia?"

"All right. What about her?" He stopped and pulled her around to face him. "Do you honestly suppose she hasn't enjoyed a good night kiss in Edinburgh on a 'brae bricht moonlit nicht'?"

"Your accent's terrible." Shyly she traced a finger down the center of his cheek. "Just so you understand how things are."

"Oh, I understand," he said kindly. "Very well, indeed. Eventually I'll go back to Sylvia and all those damned biscuits of her father's because you're in love with somebody else." He held her firmly as she would have moved away. "That's right, isn't it?"

She avoided his glance but finally she nodded.

"And it doesn't have a thing to do with money or castles or . . ."

"Or anything else," she confirmed bitterly. "And it's hopeless. He's in love with someone else . . . as you undoubtedly noticed."

He pulled her close against him. "Then don't you think we might deal very well together?" His lips brushed her temple. "At least for the moment."

Carolyn didn't bother to speak. She merely turned her face up to his and let her arms go around his neck.

Hugh didn't wait for any other answer. His kisses were gentle at first and then became demanding as his hands moved caressingly over her."

"No . . . please." Carolyn's innate honesty made her stop him.

He released her reluctantly as she pushed back from his embrace. "Sorry, Carolyn. I hope I didn't . . ."

She stopped his apology with a quick kiss on his chin. "For a minute, we both forgot Sylvia—but don't apologize anymore."

"My dear," he started to pull her close again,

"being with you is enough to make any man lose his senses."

"I'm sorry if I'm interrupting you." Mike stood barely six feet away on the path. "I thought you'd heard me coming." He reached down and retrieved the wool stole from the gravel at Carolyn's feet. "Allow me."

She snatched it away from him as he would have laid it around her shoulders. "Thanks, I can manage." Then she added irritably, "How were we supposed to hear you coming?"

"Next time I'll set off some firecrackers."

"It doesn't matter in the least," Hugh put in pacifically.

"It does to me," Carolyn contended. "With eight acres around this castle, I don't see why he has to trail our footsteps." She clutched the stole tighter around her shoulders.

"I was not trailing your footsteps," Mike assured her bleakly. "I have far better things to do. But if you don't mind, I need to see Hugh later tonight. Liz told me that you might have come down this way."

Hugh snapped his fingers. "You've just reminded me—I forgot to give Reese some instructions before we left this evening. See Carolyn back to the castle, will you, Mike? I'll be in my study when you want to talk to me." He gave Carolyn's shoulder a brief squeeze. "See you later, my dear."

Mike's glance followed him up the path. "No

wonder he's in the foreign office. There's diplomacy for you."

Carolyn was still smoldering. "You can't blame the man. Who wants to hang around in the middle of a fight?"

"I don't blame him. It's your fight . . . not his. But if you don't want to be interrupted in the middle of a necking party after this, I'd suggest you stage it somewhere other than the top of a bare cliff in the moonlight."

"You have an unholy nerve! In the first place, it wasn't a necking party and in the second place . . . any other man would have had the decency to announce himself."

Mike shoved his fists into his trouser pockets with considerable force. From his bleak look, he was obviously wishing more drastic measures could be taken. "Have it your own way," he said with resignation. "You will, anyhow. I haven't won a fight with you since I pulled you off the roadside in Bath."

"It's not from lack of trying."

"You're right about that." Now there was just plain weariness in his tone. "You can believe what you like, but I didn't mean to embarrass you with Hugh," he continued slowly. "He seems like a nice guy. Once he gets rid of his debts, he'll be in a position to offer a woman something really worthwhile."

"What has that to do with you?"

"If you'll calm down, I'll tell you."

"All right . . . I'm sorry." Her words came out with difficulty.

He responded with a faint smile. "Okay. Apology accepted. I wanted to advise you to forget about that memo paper. There's no way of knowing why Reese's nephew left it around. Apparently he didn't take the old folks into his confidence. One thing is certain, though . . . if Hugh sells the castle, you won't be staying in Wales, anyhow, so it won't matter." He stared at her preoccupied face. "You're not listening. . . ."

"Yes I am—at least to part of it. I'd just remembered where I'd heard of Reese's nephew. The doctor told me that he'd been in and out of the castle before Hugh came home."

"So?"

"Probably I'm making too much of it," she continued slowly. "Strictly woman's intuition . . . but from the doctor's tone of voice he didn't think much of the man. I wonder why?"

Mike pursed his lips and gazed down at the calm water of the bay. "I don't know. Look, Carolyn—be logical. How in the devil could we ever prove anything? You keep disregarding that point. Even if the nephew had a van like the one in Chepstow and drove it up to the front door of the castle for our inspection. I'll bet you can't remember what the driver looked like after all this time."

She let out a disheartened sigh. "Okay . . . I'll give up. If I keep on asking questions, I'll just upset Hugh—so consider the matter scratched. What happened during this week in Wales won't matter to any of us in a little while." She smiled crookedly. "It reminds me of that old television show called 'The Week That Was.' Remember?"

He started to answer her and then closed his mouth without saying anything. Slowly he fell into step beside her as they started back toward the castle. In the moonlight its stark outlines looked like a black cardboard cutout against the feathery clouds.

"Just one week out of so many," Carolyn went on, letting the words fall softly, "but I certainly won't forget it." Her voice was uneven. "Will you, Mike?"

He pulled to a stop beside her; his hands still jammed in his pockets. "No," he said roughly. "I won't forget it, Carolyn. Come on, it's getting late and I still have to talk to Hugh."

She hid her hurt at his stolid disinterest. "You go ahead. I'd like to stay outside for a while yet. Don't worry, I'll be nearby." She was concentrating on his shoes—shoes that remained stubbornly by her side. "Go on, Mike!" she said finally. "Can't you understand . . . I'd like to be left alone. For heaven's sake, don't make me spell it out."

He didn't try to answer that time—let alone comfort her. He merely walked quietly away toward the castle without looking back.

Caro took a long shuddering breath and

blinked rapidly to keep the tears from spilling over. After tomorrow, at least she wouldn't be continually upset by his physical presence. That realization, instead of comforting her as it should, caused her to dig deep in her purse for a handkerchief. Fortunately she found one and was able to mop her eyes and blow her nose. After a moment or two, she walked on aimlessly toward the side of the castle.

She remembered later that she didn't deliberately choose the route. Instead she merely followed a convenient path as her thoughts were still concerned with Mike's departure the following morning.

It took the sharp scraping of metal to make her look up in startled surprise. For a minute, the rural Welsh countryside had sounded like a busy automobile wrecking yard. She stopped and cocked her head to listen. There was a muffled thud and then the murmur of masculine voices. She was too far away to distinguish the exact words but there was no doubting the anger behind them.

Carolyn frowned and tried to peer into the shadows. The dispute must be coming from the back part of the castle; that was where an automobile would normally be parked. Her mind went quickly over the physical layout of the service wing. There was a curving drive by the kitchen and pantry areas. It was on that place that Jack the Milk parked his truck while delivering. Then there was a second driveway leading to an out-building which had been converted into garages. Mike had probably left the Vauxhall there a few minutes ago.

She flipped a mental coin and decided to see what was going on in Reese's bailiwick. She moved forward cautiously. Judging from the darkened windows at the front of the castle, all the action must be near the servants' quarters. So far, her hunch was right! At least this was one time when she could find out something for herself.

She walked on, making more noise than she would have chosen. Then the moon ducked behind a cloud and left her stranded on the edge of the path. She took a minute to get her bearings and set off again. This time she promptly walked into a prickly shrub, ruining one of her nylons in the process. The only way to go skulking in the shrubbery, she decided, was to carry a flashlight and a first-aid box.

Finally she rounded the corner of the castle and a dim light from the kitchen quarter gave shape to the object in front of her. This time there was no disputing her suspicions as her gaze lit on a familiar delivery van. It was parked close to the pantry entrance with its rear door gaping open.

She crept closer after taking care to determine that there wasn't anyone around. At last she could discover what happened at Lyonsgate so late at night.

A sudden rustle in the shrubbery by her feet caused her to jump backward with a low yelp of surprise. She stood frozen and then grimaced disgustedly when she realized she had merely frightened some tiny rodent from his lair. Her reaction was exactly like a cub scout on his first overnight hike! Next thing, she'd be imagining the ghost of the castle lurking behind the hedge.

If she needed reassuring—those weren't supernatural voices that she had heard. The profane overtone had sounded suspiciously like the twentieth century.

She crept forward to a better viewing spot, this time intent on the parked van and less aware of the nocturnal stirrings about her. Later, she decided it was this concentration which left her especially vulnerable.

When someone actually laid a heavy hand on her shoulder, she was so stunned with surprise and shock that she remained motionless for the vital minute that she might have made her escape.

By the time she finally came to life and started to scream, the hand had yanked her around and clapped a wet, sickly smelling pad over her nose and mouth. She gave a stifled gurgle and fought for breath, desperately twisting her head to shake off that pad.

Time telescoped in her mind; the sheer struggle for survival was punctuated at intervals by a panoply of roman candles exploding behind her eyelids.

Then the fireworks fizzled abruptly like a damp punk—darkness descended—and her body sagged to the ground.

Chapter Nine

What actually happened in the next hours was to forever remain a mystery. All Carolyn could truthfully claim later was that it was the most uncomfortable period she had ever spent in her life.

There were certain ingredients which were conspicuous in that discomfort whenever she came back to consciousness. It was always cold and damp—a bone-chilling damp that made her feel as if she'd been stored in the crisper box of a refrigerator.

Since she was blindfolded, bound, and gagged, it was impossible to discover where she was or who possessed the rough hands that periodically shoved her around like a sack of potatoes. Once in a while she was aware of a heated discussion in a foreign tongue, but her befogged state precluded identification of the individual voices.

The aftereffects of the anesthetic made her deathly ill and, seeing her misery, her captor eventually removed the gag.

"Keep quiet or I'll put it back," he threatened in a rough whisper. "Next time, it'll be twice as tight."

Carolyn nodded to show she understood. She was scarcely able to sit up at that moment and certainly not capable of screaming even if she'd had the chance.

A little later, she was yanked upright and pushed along an uneven walkway. Evidently her stumbling progress was too slow to suit her jailor because the sickening pad was again shoved over her nose and there was another blank space in her memory.

She felt it was years later when she roused sufficiently to feel her wrists being freed and someone fumbling with the blindfold.

"Cariad! We'll soon have you free." It was a husky masculine voice. "Try to hold on a little longer." This time the hands were gentle and a warm covering was wrapped tenderly around her shoulders.

"M'cold . . . so cold," she muttered, only partially conscious.

"You'll be warm again," the voice soothed and then she was hoisted, blanket and all, against a broad chest. "Just as soon as I can get you back to the castle."

Her eyes fluttered open but she could only see the barest outline of a head above her. "Hugh?" She mouthed the name with difficulty. "Hugh ... please take me home."

"Soon ... cariad." For a moment he rested his cheek against the top of her head to comfort her.

Poor Hugh, she thought incoherently. Then it was too much trouble to think or talk or do anything except relax in his strong arms.

The next time she opened her eyes she was in her room at the castle and there was a familiar pattern of sunlight streaming across the coverlet.

She started to sit up and fell back with a groan.

Liz was up like a shot from her chair by the fireplace. "Caro darling ... what is it? Are you all right?"

The other pushed up on an elbow and focused on Liz's anxious face. "I didn't mean to startle you." Her glance darkened with apprehension. "Liz—I *am* here, aren't I? I mean ... here in the castle with you?"

"I know what you mean, sweetie," Liz cut in comfortingly. "You're here and you're going to be fine as soon as you have a little more rest. Your favorite Scottish doctor called in the gray light of dawn to look you over."

Carolyn rubbed her forehead. It was a tossup whether her headache from the night before was worse than the prickling ache of the bump over her ear caused by the rock slide. "At the moment," she said ruefully, "I feel like a fugitive from Blue Cross."

"Well, the doctor said it was nice you had a thickish skull because a person evidently needed one for a visit to Lyonsgate. Then he told Hugh not to bother to invite him for the weekend because he didn't think he was strong enough to stand the pace." She smiled. "I think he was partly serious. Hugh will have to explain things or the villagers will be ostracizing him."

Carolyn pushed a pillow behind her back and decided that the world was settling down. She wished she could say as much for the state of her stomach. "I feel awful," she proclaimed dismally.

Liz sat on the edge of the bed and patted her hand. "I know, dear—that's what happens after ether. The doctor said your stomach would be upset. How about some tea? I just brought some up from the kitchen."

Carolyn considered the possibilities. "It will either kill or cure," she said finally, "but anything would be better than this. I'll try a cup." She watched Liz move over to the low table in front of the fireplace to pour it. Her gaze went down to the hearth and then flashed up again. "Liz—where's Poppa Bear?"

The teapot almost landed in the middle of the china. "Who? Oh, you mean the rug. I suppose one of the cleaning women put it back in Mike's room. That's where it belongs, isn't it?"

"I guess so." She couldn't explain that she missed the bedraggled specimen—that he was a link with something beloved and familiar. Gloomily she pushed back into her pillow and took the cup of tea Liz handed her. "It's probably full of moths," she said, trying to be sensible.

"Mike's room? I shouldn't think so. The cleaning women do a wonderful job considering the acres they have to cover."

"I meant the bearskin." She sipped her tea and frowned as if it were poisoned hemlock. The way she felt it would have been in keeping. "He could at least show some interest whether I live or die," she burst out finally.

"The bear!" Liz gave her a worried look and edged toward the bathroom door. "I'll get a cold cloth for your head."

"Come back...." Carolyn waved a restraining hand, almost upsetting her tea in the process. "Stop acting as if I'm a case. I'm talking about Mike, of course."

Liz turned around and put her hands on her hips. "Of course," she said with some sarcasm. "I'm sorry the doctor didn't stay longer. He could have added an entire page to his case notes on mental patients. And I'm talking about Carolyn Drummond, in case you're wondering."

"I thought you were," Caro said without offense, and took another sip of tea. She decided the steaming liquid had been a good idea, after all. If she continued improving at this rate, she could soon get up and dress.

Liz was evidently reading her mind. "Don't get any notions about leaving your bed of pain. The doctor's coming back this afternoon to sign your walking papers. Until then, you stay put."

Carolyn subsided. "If you say so. But Liz—I want to go home."

"Considering what's happened—I don't blame you." The older woman took Carolyn's empty cup and put it on the tea tray before she moved over and sat on the end of the bed. "Besides, now that Henry's no longer interested in the castle, we should leave Hugh in peace. I'm confused, though. I thought Hugh had offered you a lifetime invitation to Lyonsgate."

"Hugh's been in Burma too long. When he finally sinks his pride over finances, he'll fly back to his Sylvia in Scotland." Carolyn plucked a piece of lint from the bedspread and carefully put it in an ashtray. "I just happened along to help him over a bad patch. It was good for both of us."

"Your version doesn't quite tally with the story I've heard from other parts. Are you sure that's the way it is?"

Carolyn avoided looking up. "That's the way it's going to be," she said lightly but definitely. "How's the room service in this place? The tea worked miracles but I'm ready for a second course."

"You surprise me." Liz got to her feet. "I was

sure you'd be dying with curiosity to hear what happened. Instead, all you want to do is eat a boiled egg and take the first train back to London."

Carolyn did look up then. Her eyes were still shadowed from the night's ordeal, but her gaze was clear. "That's right, Liz—and that's exactly what I'm going to do. Whether Henry likes it or not."

"Don't rush your fences, Caro. . . ." A gentle rap on the hall door cut ino her words. "I'll bet I know who that is," she said with some relief and went over to open it.

Carolyn sat up straighter and thought, "It's about time he showed up!"

"Hugh!" Liz said happily. "Thank goodness you've come. The invalid's getting fractious and I need your help."

Bleakness washed over Carolyn's face and she slumped back down on her pillows.

"Is she all right?" Hugh was asking in a tone reserved for hospital corridors.

"Practically as good as new," the patient told him. "Come in, please. My only trouble now is that I'm hungry. I've been bullying Liz to order some breakfast."

"Now that you're here to keep watch on her, I'll do just that," Liz replied. "I'll even bring an extra pot of coffee for us, Hugh."

He glanced up from dragging an upholstered chair to the bedside. "Good! But I hope you'll make it yourself. The Welsh aren't dab hands at brewing the stuff."

"Mrs. Reese could take a few lessons. . . ." Carolyn agreed.

"Oh, but she isn't . . ." Liz broke off as her gaze met Hugh's and she retreated toward the door in confusion. "I'll be back in a little while with your breakfast, Caro." She fluttered out, closing the door behind her.

"What was that all about?" Carolyn asked Hugh. As he hesitated, she added firmly, "I think it's time you told me what's going on around here. And you can skip that 'frail little woman' attitude."

A sudden grin lighted his face. "Dear girl, I wouldn't dare. Both you and Liz frighten me dreadfully. It must be something to do with American women."

She snorted. "Translated that means you'll tell me exactly what you've decided I should hear . . . and nothing more. Right?"

"As a former Queen's Scout, a member of Her Majesty's Foreign Service, and a solid British gentleman—I'll tell you whatever you want to know. Within certain limitations, of course."

"I knew that was all I could hope for," she said with a faint smile. "All right . . . brace yourself for the deluge. How did you know I was missing in the first place?"

"The credit for that goes to Mike," he said, crossing his long legs and getting comfortable. "It goes against my instincts to admit it, but he was the one who set off the alarm. Not literally, my dear, but most effectively nonetheless. He routed me out of bed and complained that you couldn't be found anywhere. By that time, he had already searched the castle grounds looking for you and discovered the van belonging to Reese's nephew parked behind the old stable wing."

"Reese's nephew!" Surprise widened her eyes. "So he *was* the one all along."

"Yes indeed." Hugh rested his head against the back of his chair. "Definitely the villain of the piece—a nasty bit of goods."

Carolyn bit her lip to keep from laughing at his solemn pronouncement. "If he's the one who shoved that smelly pad in my face and made me sick to my stomach for the next eight hours—he's certainly a ring-tailed stinker!"

"Er . . . yes." Hugh looked slightly embarrassed at her fervent declaration. "No question about it."

"Did you find him in the van?"

He shook his head. "No . . . there wasn't a soul around when Mike went through it. Nor was there anything in it. That was the key to everything, you see."

"The van?"

"Oh, no. The cargo he was carrying around in the van at various times."

She wrinkled her forehead. "I feel as if I'm

playing twenty questions. Do you mean it was stolen cargo?"

He hitched forward in his chair. "No. The merchandise was paid for, but that was the only legal thing about it. The smuggling of arms is definitely frowned on by Her Majesty's customs."

Carolyn's mouth dropped open. "Good lord," she said finally, "I hadn't even thought of that angle. But why was he smuggling arms into Wales? I thought the national extremist group here had outlawed violence."

"You're right about that. Actually you have to look at a map to get the answer but it's right across St. George's Channel."

"Ireland?" Her lips mouthed the word unbelievingly. "Of course, smuggled arms for Ireland. With all the strife in Northern Ireland, there would be a ready market for contraband."

"Unfortunately . . . yes."

"And the fishing boat . . ." her thoughts were racing ahead. "That's how they were being transported, wasn't it?"

He nodded. "But don't ask me whether they were going to the Irish Republic or Northern Ireland because the British authorities aren't answering any questions on that score. They *do* admit they're delighted to have broken part of the smuggling ring. Just last month, the Dutch police seized some Czech-made weapons aboard a plane in Amsterdam. The month before, Irish customs' men in the Republic found a shipment of trunks containing submachine guns and grenades being unloaded from a passenger liner." He pointed a finger for emphasis. "Those had been shipped from New York."

"I had no idea...."

"It was a shock to me, too. Just because Wales is the nearest neighbor to Ireland, it never occurred to me that they'd be using our sea caves for smuggling again. It was better in the old days when they concentrated on French brandy and velvet."

"Heavens yes!" She shifted restlessly on her pillow. "Was Reese's nephew gunrunning when I saw him at Chepstow?"

"Evidently. He didn't want anyone peering into the van to see his 'cheese' shipment. Reese was his passenger that time, by the way. It was a shock for him when you turned up at Lyonsgate two days later."

"I can imagine. Too bad his nephew didn't make a better job of it."

"From what they say, there were no sinister overtones to your accident. They merely wanted to get out of there ... fast. Earlier, they had picked up the crates of arms at the docks in Cardiff. The contraband came with some very legal shipments of cheese ordered by the Wellington Foods Company for sale in England. Cheese was an ideal cover-up for the customs inspection. After several legitimate crates were checked, the rest of the shipments would come in without any trouble.

The smugglers were smart enough to direct the incoming arms shipments to various ports in Britain and Wales so that no one would get suspicious. Since Reese's nephew worked for Wellington Foods, he was able to combine his two sources of income very nicely. Apparently the officers of the company were completely innocent, but a number of them have very red faces today after this disclosure. I'd hate to be the man who hired young Reese."

"He's probably halfway to New Zealand by now with a one-way ticket."

"I imagine you're right. British customs will certainly be interested in all cheese shipments coming to the country for the next few months. Even the cheddar will end up looking like Swiss cheese after they finish testing it."

She gave a sympathetic chuckle. "No doubt. I'm still not clear on their smuggling procedure, though. Where did they store the cargo while they were waiting to take it across to Ireland?"

"Where else but convenient, deserted Lyonsgate Castle." His lips thinned in disgust. "How do you think I feel about that!"

"But you weren't here until last week. . . ."

"That's my only excuse *and* alibi, thank God. Reese was the one who was made to cooperate. Unfortunately the old man was arrested for smuggling years ago. The nephew apparently threatened to expose his record unless Reese helped him in this scheme. Since I wasn't around, the old fellow evidently took the easiest way out. Then, unluckily, I returned home. Worse still . . ."

". . . you were invaded by a bunch of nosy house guests," she finished for him. "I was impolite enough to even hear noises the first night."

"Something like that," he conceded.

"But how could I hear anything from the kitchen wing way up here?"

"They weren't moving those guns around in the kitchen," he said. "They were using parts of the old smugglers' tunnel for storage. It winds behind the walls of the castle and carries any noise like a sounding board."

"I thought the tunnels and passageways were boarded up long ago."

"They were . . . until recently. Unfortunately, young Reese knew they'd make an ideal cache for storing contraband. All he had to do was knock out a few bricks and they were in business. Even his regular appearances at Lyonsgate wouldn't excite any comment. His uncle could just tell the villagers that his nephew was visiting again. Most people don't look for trouble," Hugh went on. "Frankly, I wouldn't have thought of suspecting Reese until Mike got the wind up."

Mike again. Carolyn wished fervently that Hugh would keep him out of the conversation. Even the mention of his name was enough to make her nerves twang like a violin string.

She pushed at the pillow, which was now slipping down behind her shoulders and changed the subject slightly. "Was Reese cooperative when you finally cornered him?"

"We couldn't find him, at first. Maybe it was a blessing because we were able to deal with Mrs. Reese. When I told her that we'd have to call in the police, she promptly collapsed in hysterics. After that, she couldn't talk fast enough. From what I could understand of her Welsh, she hadn't wanted to help the nephew in the first place. Then young Wyn ... as they called him ... got tough. He threatened to expose his uncle's past criminal record, so the old people were afraid not to submit. Mrs. Reese wasn't so keen on telling what had happened to you." Hugh scratched absently at his eyebrow. "She must have sensed that they were in real trouble there. About then, Mike noticed that cat of hers frisking around her feet. It made him think that there was a chance the cat had gotten down in the cave through a tunnel from the castle." He looked at her reproachfully. "I didn't even know the cat had been in the cave. You didn't mention it to me on the way back."

"I'm sorry," she said, properly meek. "I guess I was thinking of something else."

He didn't answer directly but his expression spoke volumes. "Anyhow," he said finally, "there was nothing for it then but to go chasing down to the beach and try to retrace the cat's journey. But by that time the tide was in and we had to wait for it to turn so we could get around to the cave.

Just as we were finally starting up the beach, we caught sight of the fishing boat raising anchor and hoisting their dinghy aboard. That's when we took time out to call the police and bring them up to date. From the bare bones Mrs. Reese told us, they loaded contraband from the cave and we wanted to set the Coastal Watch after them before they could get outside territorial waters."

"Were you successful?"

"Oh yes." He was almost smug. "The crew of the fishing boat had no reason to suspect anything was wrong, you see. When British custom's men boarded it in midchannel, they even found young Reese. He was going to Ireland to collect his money. Then, after a day or so, he would merely have taken a channel ferry back into Fishguard and gotten on an express train to London so he could report back to his job."

"What was he going to do about me?" Carolyn asked indignantly.

"His uncle was set to discover your unconscious body on the castle grounds this morning. Since you hadn't seen anything, you couldn't have testified who your assailant was. I rather imagine young Wyn hoped you would be in poor physical condition after a night in that damp tunnel."

He left unspoken the thought in both their minds—that a few more hours in the tunnel and Carolyn wouldn't have testified to anything again . . . ever.

She compressed her lips to stop their sudden

trembling and avoided looking at Hugh's bleak face. "I was right about the boat, then," she said after a moment's pause. "I knew it shouldn't be so close to shore that afternoon."

"I heard the story about that when I talked to the police a few minutes ago. The fishing boat captain admitted he was waiting for a signal from Wyn Reese regarding their pickup. When the younger Reese saw you down on the path, he thought he could scare you off with a rock slide. According to the police, he felt you were a jinx from the very beginning."

"Our admiration was mutual," she said dryly. "I was beginning to wish that I'd never set foot in Wales."

Hugh's face softened and he shifted quickly from his chair to the edge of the bed. "I'm awfully glad you did, Carolyn." There was an undercurrent of pure happiness in his voice. "Everything has turned out so well that I think the luck of the Lyons has changed at last. How would you like to keep company with an Englishman who has finally shed his family albatross?"

She reached out to clasp his hand. "Hugh! You've sold the castle!"

He nodded. "I can scarcely believe it myself."

"But that's wonderful! I've felt so guilty ever since old Henry changed his mind. So has Liz."

"There was no need to. Actually, if you hadn't come—I would never have made this deal."

Her hand fell back. "I don't understand. Did Henry change his mind again?"

He shook his head. "No, I meant that without you—Mike would never have heard about Lyonsgate Castle."

"What the dickens does Mike have to do with it?" she burst out.

"My God, Carolyn—he's the one who bought it." He saw her stupefied look and hastened to explain. "Oh, not for himself. He doesn't have that kind of money personally, but his employers do." Hugh leaned back to rest against the post at the foot of the bed. "Piles and piles of American dollars for investing in hotels all over the world. That's why Mike was across the Atlantic in the first place. He'd been down in Italy checking on their newest hotel in Capri. Apparently he's the executive they send around whenever the balance sheet doesn't look right."

"I thought he was a tennis bum," she murmured abstractedly.

"My dear, I can't imagine why. Just because he wanted to see the Wimbledon tournament as long as he was in England. . . ."

"Don't you start defending him, too."

"This morning I'd fight a duel for him. Imagine all that money for this pile of stone! He even checked with the village council on the zoning restrictions and had the whole thing ready to go when he called his boss from Tenby. I've heard from their London branch this morning and the papers will be here for signing this afternoon." His eyes lit up. "I could even quit the Foreign Office if I liked."

"Don't do anything rash," she cautioned. "Now that you're used to rice, Hong Kong might look pretty good in a week or so."

He sat upright. "With a wife, it would look much better. You don't have to have that dowry now, Carolyn."

She smiled faintly. "Look out! You're almost stepping on the flypaper."

"Good!" He reached over to recapture her hand. "What about it? There isn't any moonlight, but I don't think we need it."

"Hugh dearest, you could be persuasive in the middle of a sandstorm in the Sahara desert at high noon."

He edged forward still further. "Stop being diplomatic and skirting the issue."

"I'm not being diplomatic . . . just realistic. The first time I cooked breakfast for you, our marriage would be in trouble. Liz will tell you I can barely scramble an egg—much less steam a bloater. What *is* a bloater, anyway?"

"I don't think I'll answer that." His mouth softened in a fond smile. "At least give me a few more days, Carolyn dear. Mrs. Reese is staying on here for a bit. She could serve as chaperone if Liz can't stay with you."

She parried for time. "What happens to Mrs. Reese's husband in the meantime?"

"That's up to the authorities. For now, he's been released to their cottage on the grounds until the case comes up."

"How did he manage that?"

"I told them I'd be responsible." He brushed it off and moved to a safer topic. "The police superintendent wants you to sign a statement today as soon as the doctor gives his okay."

"Of course." Her eyebrows drew together as she frowned. "I'm sorry to cause trouble for old Reese. After all, he was just a pawn in all this."

"Don't be too charitable. Even after Wyn was on the fishing boat, you were still freezing in the tunnel. Reese wasn't doing anything about it when I intercepted him."

Her cheeks flushed at the remembrance of that rescue. "Hugh," she asked suddenly, "what does 'cariad' mean?"

He seemed taken aback. "Cariad? I didn't know you were studying Welsh, Carolyn. It's a term of endearment ... 'darling, dear, dearest,' take your pick." Grinning, he added, "Very handy if you stay in the neighborhood."

"I should imagine." She decided his use of the word in the tunnel must have been an outpouring of affectionate relief. Evidently he'd forgotten that he'd even said it.

"Cariad ..." He mouthed it appreciatively as he watched her. "It fits you nicely. Tell me, cariad ... are you going to take pity on me and stay at Lyonsgate?"

She shook her head. "Sorry, Hugh. I'm one of the working class. It's time for me to go back home and ask for a salary raise after this hazardous overseas duty."

He released her hand and stood up. "I don't understand. You're determined to treat the whole thing as a joke."

Her glance pleaded with him. "After all that's happened, I'd burst out crying if I didn't take it lightly. You don't have to tell me that I should accept your proposal. You're tremendously good-looking, a marvelous companion ... you even have a title to dangle in front of a woman, and who could resist that?"

"I know of one woman," he said dryly. "And you can stop giving testimonials. Even in Britain, we don't like to hear that this can be the beginning of a splendid friendship."

"If I stayed at Lyonsgate any longer, it would probably be the beginning of a splendid affair," she said, owning up to the truth. "You're much too persuasive."

"Darling! I knew you'd be honest about it. . . ."

She smiled at his elated pronouncement but shook her head. "Slow down, Hugh. That's why I'm not staying. I owed you the truth, but I'm not going to follow through. Not even in the mood I'm in. Go on up to Scotland—and you be honest with Sylvia. If you're determined to have a last fling, detour by London on the way."

His stare was frankly reflective. "I'm not sure I

approve of your advice but I'll consider it." He bent down then and kissed her cheek softly. "No matter what happens, Carolyn ... I won't forget these days with you." His next words came more slowly. "Are you sure you didn't give Mike the wrong idea? I could have sworn he thought you were somebody else's property."

"Then you misunderstood. He was the one wearing the 'sold' sign." At his uncomprehending look, she could only shake her head again helplessly. "Never mind, Hugh. I'll survive ... but thanks for your kind thoughts."

"If you should change your mind, a box of rice sent in care of the Foreign Office will reach me."

She smiled. "I won't forget."

There was a thud at the hall door.

"That must be Liz with your breakfast," he said, moving over to let her in.

"Before you go, Hugh," Carolyn said hastily, "I want to officially thank you for rescuing me last night. It was like a miracle when you carried me out of that tunnel. I think I'd given up hope."

Hugh had opened the door but he turned to give her a perturbed look. Even Liz, coming over the threshold, hesitated before she walked in and put the breakfast tray on a bedside table.

Carolyn sat bolt upright. "Now what? You both look as if I'd said something awful."

Liz shook her head. "Not awful, Caro."

"I guess we didn't make it clear, darling," Hugh put in easily. "When we found old Reese down by the cave, I felt responsible for getting him to the authorities." He shrugged. "I wasn't the one who carried you out."

"Who was it then?" Her toneless question was almost rhetorical and they all knew it.

Hugh made an apologetic gesture. "It was Mike who did the honors. I told him he had all the luck."

Carolyn wasn't listening to his last words. She turned abruptly to Liz. "Well, why hasn't he come to see me, then? Can't he take a few minutes from his business transactions to be decently polite?" She slipped her hands under the blanket to hide their trembling. "You can tell him that I won't take much of his time."

Liz had paled during the tirade. "It's no use, Caro. I can't tell him."

"Why not?" The stark words were filled with longing.

Hugh spoke up softly. "Because he's gone, my dear. He packed his bags and left Lyonsgate early this morning. He made a special point of asking me to tell you goodbye."

Chapter Ten

"Listen Caro," Liz said later in some concern, "you'll have to stop crying or the doctor will keep you here for days." She would have appealed for reinforcements, but Hugh, manlike, had beat a hasty retreat at the first sign of tears. "Besides," Liz added cannily, "your egg is getting cold."

"Damn the egg!" Carolyn got out between sobs.

"All right, then. You can eat it chilly and hard-boiled. There's no need to worry about the toast." She gave the chrome toast rack a baleful glance. "It's cold already."

"I don't want any toast."

"You'll eat it anyway," Liz said. She strolled over to the window and peered out. "I think it's going to be a nice day for a change. As soon as we're ready to leave this country, the sun comes out. I wonder if there's a message in that?" She turned purposefully back toward the bed. "Carolyn—we've wasted enough time. I want to talk to you, but first, take this clean handkerchief and blow your nose."

Caro put out a grudging hand and buried her nose in the square of cambric.

"That's better," said Liz. "Now—dry your eyes. At your age you should know that crying won't get you anywhere. Besides, I'm darned if I know why you turned on the waterworks. I thought you were all set for my blessing with Hugh. Did I have the right maps but the wrong battlefield?"

Carolyn was still trying to stifle her sobs. "I don't know how you could have been so silly. There was nothing really serious between Hugh and me. In a day or so, he'll recognize what a lucky escape he's had."

"Don't talk nonsense. It would have been a very suitable match. Even Henry approved of it."

"Liz! How could you say such a thing."

"I merely mentioned it in the course of our telephone conversation." The older woman made an airy gesture. "Once he got over the initial shock, he rallied pretty well. Naturally he didn't approve of your living in Hong Kong, but he probably could have adjusted to it."

"Naturally," Carolyn said dryly. "Well, he won't have to worry now, but don't ever let Hugh hear of it."

"I wasn't going to print a newspaper," Liz answered in some heat. "Really, Carolyn, you're certainly acting strangely today. What's all the fuss about Mike? You knew he was going."

"Of course I did. Let's not go over it blow by blow." Carolyn's tone was resigned. "I'd better eat my egg now."

Liz nodded in the direction of the tray. "Help yourself . . . but I'm not changing the subject. Surely you weren't upset when you heard that his company bought Lyonsgate? I thought it was a wonderful break for Hugh."

"I know it was, but you can't blame me for being surprised. I hadn't thought of Mike being a businessman. He always seemed so casual about things."

"Mike?" Liz exhibited sheer amazement. "Then you didn't look very closely. When that man wanted something, he reminded me of a Siamese fighting fish going after a brine shrimp. Whammo! No hanky-panky, no indecision—just an accomplished fact." She leaned against the bedpost and smiled dreamily. "I like a man who acts like that."

Carolyn swallowed a bite of egg before saying, "It isn't so good if you're the brine shrimp."

"Were you?" The question was slipped in softly.

Her patient did look up then, but just for a second. "I didn't mean to be. After the first day or so, I couldn't help myself." She toyed with the spoon on her saucer. "Now it's too late."

"Because you fell in love with him."

Carolyn shrugged. "It's too late because he's gone back to his redheaded girlfriend after a week's fling in Wales. And he was such a damned gentleman all the time he was here that he won't even have to apologize to her."

Liz was frowning. "Do you mean you're having this trauma because Mike is supposed to love some Italian beauty?"

"One beauty in particular. Her name is Gina."

"Oh my lord," Liz clung to her bedpost for support. "Didn't he explain to you?"

Caro rubbed her forehead as she said, "Look ... am I the patient or are you? I don't know what you're talking about."

"I'm talking," Liz said, biting off her words deliberately, "about Michael Evans' Italian love life. I don't know what silly name he told you but the one it generally goes by is Ferrari. All this time he's been talking about his brand new, bright red, very expensive Italian sports car. He just bought it when he was in Naples on this trip."

Carolyn looked like an astonished owl. "You're kidding," she breathed finally. "You have to be kidding."

"I don't kid about important things. It never occurred to me that he hadn't told you the truth."

"But how did you find out?"

"He had a picture from an advertising brochure in his wallet. It fluttered out the day I borrowed some money from him to pay Jack the Milk." Her lips quirked comically. "You know men when they get to talking about new cars. I thought the milkman would never leave. He's always wanted a Ferrari, too. Darned if he didn't insist on shaking Mike's hand to congratulate him."

"That sneaking, miserable prevaricator. . . ."

"The milkman?" Liz queried innocently.

Carolyn ignored that sally. "He led me on all this time and didn't even have the decency to tell the truth."

"Hey . . . wait a minute. Mike explained that to me. When he first met you, he thought that you'd feel safer with him if he had a fiancée somewhere in the background. He said the only name he could think of was Gina."

"Undoubtedly from a classical reading list," Carolyn said bitterly. She was remembering how she had been convinced by his play upon words. "He must have had a wonderful time laughing at me. Why didn't he tell the truth later on? Surely there wasn't any need for pretense after we got to the castle."

"By that time, the lord of the manor had appeared. He thought you'd fallen in love with Hugh."

"I tried to give that impression for self-defense," Carolyn wailed. "What else could I do when I remembered Gina?"

Liz shook her head in despair. "I don't see how two people could manage such a muddle."

Caro agreed. "After he told you the true story, he undoubtedly thought you'd tell me. . . ."

"And I was sure the idiot would make a beeline to settle the matter himself. If I'd used my head, I would have remembered that there isn't a man alive who likes to make lengthy explanations."

"So when I didn't show any interest in him after that, he thought I was telling him to get lost. Oh lord . . ." Carolyn clapped her hand to her mouth.

"What now?"

"I just remembered. When he kissed me in the cave—I was awful. It's a wonder I didn't slap his face. . . . I did everything else."

"No wonder the poor man left early this morning." Liz saw the crestfallen expression on the other's face and said hurriedly, "Don't worry, honey, now that you know it was a misunderstanding—you can straighten it out."

"No, I can't. You can talk about Women's Lib all you want, but I can't go chasing after Mike just because he kissed me once."

"Don't be a nit. Remember that he dragged you back here twice—clutched to his manly chest both times. A man doesn't do that unless he has more than a passing interest."

"He couldn't do anything else around here," Caro said dismally. "This isn't the place to call for an aid car." But even as she spoke she was remembering that whispered endearment when he found her in the tunnel—wondering if his soft "cariad" was something he would have bestowed on any woman.

She turned her head restlessly, resenting the blanket of depression that had settled over her. Why must she feel only half-alive—feel that life would never be exactly right again—just because one man had gone away. She drew a deep breath, realizing there was a dreadful finality about those last two words. But a woman would have to be sensible; she couldn't chase after a man and ask if he had any honorable intentions ... or even dishonorable ones. Besides, Mike hadn't left a forwarding address unless Liz knew of one.

She took another deep breath and decided it wouldn't hurt to ask.

Liz watched the panoply of emotions chase over Carolyn's face and wished she could help her. Unfortunately Mike had been so offhand when he had said goodbye that it was difficult to know exactly what was in his mind.

". . . so do you think it would be all right, Liz?"

"Sorry." Liz came back to the present. "Would what be all right?"

"I wondered if it would be proper to write him a note?"

The older woman made a clucking noise with her tongue. "Proper! Good heavens, you're in the wrong generation with that word. You'll never get a man that way."

Carolyn blushed. "I'm not setting a trap . . ." she began.

"That's good, because there isn't time," Liz finished for her.

"Isn't Mike going to the Wimbledon tournament?"

"He's changed his plans. When Mike folds his tent and steals away, he does it with a vengeance! He's taking the first ship to New York. His boat train leaves Waterloo tomorrow morning."

"Oh God." Carolyn sank back against her pillows as if she'd been beaten. "Then he can't care at all," she murmured, barely loud enough to be heard. "It was just another weekend for him."

"I'm not sure of that," Liz said suddenly. "I'd almost forgotten that he left you something. Have another cup of tea while I run to my room and get it. I'd packed it away because I thought it would never be needed."

Carolyn's pale cheeks took on a vestige of color. "Wait a minute! Don't run off until you explain. . . ."

Liz barely hesitated while wrenching open the heavy hall door. "I'll be back in two shakes . . . then you can explain it to me."

Actually it was three minutes by the little French clock on Carolyn's bedside table before Liz came back with a paper-wrapped package. Without bothering to unwrap it, she thrust it into Carolyn's hands and watched her tear off the covering like a six-year-old undoing a birthday present.

"Liz . . . look! He left the Sweetheart Spoon!" She raised a shining glance to the other. "Tell me exactly what he said when he gave it to you."

"Let's see . . . Mike handed it over the very last thing. Almost as if he'd second thoughts on the idea. He didn't tell me what it was; he merely said that if you decided not to marry Hugh, he'd like you to have it." She wrinkled her forehead as she concentrated. "Then he said something about hoping you'd hang it in the window."

"Did he really! How wonderful! Oh . . . let me out of here." Caro was so excited that she couldn't push back the twisted sheet with one hand while clutching her precious Sweetheart Spoon with the other. "I have to get dressed. When's the first train to London?"

"Carolyn Drummond! Get back in that bed right now," Liz commanded. "You're not to wriggle a toe until the doctor comes and gives his permission. I mean it."

"Then he'd better hurry up," her patient threatened, "because I'm going to be in London tomorrow morning if I have to arrive in my pajamas."

"The way fashions are today, you wouldn't raise an eyebrow. Don't worry though—there's plenty of time. The doctor will be along shortly and he shouldn't be hard to convince. You look like a different person already." Her eyes sparkled. "There must be witchcraft connected with that Sweetheart Spoon."

"There is . . . but only if the right person gives it to you," Caro assured her. She sank back against the pillows and beamed. "I've never felt so happy in my life—I think I'll kiss the next man who walks in."

"That's a fine way to talk. Wait until I tell Michael about this reaction!"

There was a faint rapping on the door. After a discreet pause, the door was thrust open so one of Hugh's "dailies" could stick her head around it.

"Begging your pardon, miss. There's a gentleman waiting in the hall to see you."

Carolyn looked challengingly at Liz. "I'll bet the doctor would be charmed if his patient kissed him."

"You wouldn't!" Liz tried to look severe.

"Want to bet?"

The cleaning woman watched their lighthearted exchange with wide eyes. It was hard to believe that the vibrant young woman on the bed was the patient she'd heard about. From the rumor in the village, the poor soul was in death's shadow after that nasty business in the tunnel last night. Now, here she was sitting up and looking like a peck of mischief as she carried on with Mrs. Sheppard.

Liz folded her arms imperiously. "Ten American dollars say you wouldn't dare."

"It's a shame to fleece you but you're on." Carolyn turned her laughing gaze back to the cleaning woman. "Will you ask the doctor to come in, please."

The other started to withdraw and then turned back to say anxiously, "But it's not the doctor, miss, it's the police inspector." She looked at Liz. "Shall I fetch him in, Mrs. Sheppard?"

"By all means . . . send the police inspector in." Liz doubled over with laughter as she stared at Carolyn's stricken face. "I wouldn't miss this for anything!"

She was still chuckling about it hours later as their train pulled into London in the gritty light of dawn. When the gray outlines of Paddington Station became visible and they started gathering their luggage she said, "I need that extra ten dollars to help my morale at this point. If you ever convince me to get on a midnight milk train of British Railways again, it'll be because I'm bound and gagged."

"You were an angel to come along," Carolyn said, peering uneasily out the window. "I was afraid to risk taking a later train, but I didn't know this one delivered the morning papers as well as the milk."

Both women had been sorry to miss seeing more of Wales' rolling hills and grassy dells with their night journey. Even the heavily populated industrial centers of Swansea and Cardiff had merely been isolated clusters of flickering lights. At the deserted train stations, alighting passengers had scurried down the long concrete platforms and disappeared like gophers ducking into a burrow. The few courageous travelers who had boarded the train promptly propped themselves in corners of their compartments and dozed fitfully. Carolyn had thought the night would never end and as they finally neared London, she was appalled to learn how late their arrival was going to be.

She looked at her watch again and said worriedly, "There won't be time for me to get cleaned up in the hotel. If I can find a taxi, I'll head straight for Waterloo Station. What a pity we didn't know where Mike was staying so we could have left a message for him."

Liz agreed as she struggled into her camel's hair topcoat. "And if we could have caught an earlier train, we wouldn't have this thrash. It's a shame you had to wait at Lyonsgate to sign that police statement."

"It wasn't anyone's fault. When Wyn Reese decided to confess and started naming the other members of the smuggling syndicate, it delayed things. The inspector explained that they wanted to check his last statement against mine to make sure the salient facts agreed. Otherwise, they would have questioned him further."

"I still can't see why you didn't press charges against his uncle."

Carolyn fiddled with the catch on her handbag. "It was mainly because of the way Mrs. Reese looked when I saw her at the police station. The poor woman must have cried all night."

Liz's usually cheerful features settled into grim lines. "I know, and she doesn't have much to look forward to even now. You can't blame Hugh for wanting to sell Lyonsgate—that place seems to attract tragedy. What a homecoming for him after those years in Burma."

"Well, his visit to Scotland should redeem everything," Carolyn said, smiling. "He told me that Sylvia can scarcely wait until he gets up there. I knew he was being too casual about her all along."

Liz nodded. "They'll probably announce their engagement next month. Now that Hugh has sold the castle, he can stop being stuffy about finances. I'm glad that he's coming to London later this week, so he can give us the latest word on his love life. Make sure you persuade Mike to cancel his ship reservation and stay over here for a while. There's no sense in his going off like this."

"I'll try—but you know Mike. He has a mind of his own. This time though, I'm going to be hanging onto his coattails wherever he goes." She crossed her fingers. "If I only get the chance."

Liz leaned down to peep through a grimy window as the train rolled slowly into the station. "You'd better fly for a taxi as soon as this miserable conveyance stops. Otherwise, you'll miss the boat train and end up by chartering a small plane

245

to Southampton. I don't know how we'd explain that item on the expense account."

"What about our luggage? You'll never be able to manage alone."

"Nonsense! If I can't get out of a London train station by myself, I'm ready for an old folk's home." She clutched the door of their compartment as the train jolted to a stop. "Leave a message for me at the hotel when you find out what your young man has decided. Now ..." she slid open the glass barrier leading to the corridor. "Scoot!"

Carolyn scooted.

She tore down the almost-empty platform toward the taxi rank at the side of the station and luckily found a yawning cabby who had just disgorged his passenger.

"Waterloo Station and hurry, please," she instructed, climbing into the back seat. "I have to make a boat train."

The cabby looked up at the station clock and shook his head doubtfully. "You've left it pretty late, miss. It's a good thing there's not much traffic." He shifted into low, cutting directly in front of an oncoming vehicle and causing another approaching from the right to come to a shuddering halt.

Carolyn gasped as he accelerated out onto the street. After that, she tried to keep her eyes lowered for the next fifteen minutes as the cab wove into Bayswater Road, then down Park Lane, where the lush greenery of Hyde Park was coming to life alongside, and finally onto Grosvenor Place behind the grounds of Buckingham Palace.

At the curbside, lumbering double-deck buses known affectionately as "Red Rovers" were methodically picking up passengers from neat serpentine queues. Beyond them, metropolitan shopkeepers were just starting to wash their display windows. As the taxi turned past Westminster Abbey and the stately Houses of Parliament, Big Ben began tolling the hour directly above them.

The driver caught Carolyn's worried glance in the rear-vision mirror and said consolingly, "Not to worry, miss. Be there in half a tick now."

When they pulled up at the busy station, Carolyn had the fare ready. As soon as the car stopped, she shoved a bill into the driver's hand.

"Thanks so much," she said breathlessly.

He nodded. "Through those doors, miss—and run!"

He sounded just like Liz, she thought irrelevantly, and she ran. Past the porters with their luggage carts, past the slow-moving passengers who were taking a later train, past the busy newsstand with books piled high. All the while she was trying to sort out the huge illuminated departure board at the far end of the concourse. Then she caught sight of the magic words "Boat Train" posted on track three and ran frantically toward it just as the ticket-taker started closing the metal gate.

He didn't try to stop her. He waved her on, shouting, "Jump in the first car past the baggage—the train's leaving now. Run!"

She ran.

She whizzed past the baggage car and waved desperately at a uniformed brakeman who was standing on the platform steps signaling the engineer.

He gave her a startled glance before calling, "Come on, lass—over here!" As she panted up, he reached out to haul her aboard at the precise moment the train started to move. "Are ye' all right?" he asked in a broad Scottish accent as she collapsed against the end of the coach.

She was too out of breath to answer but she smiled gamely and nodded.

He patted her shoulder in friendly fashion and closed the vestibule door as the train gathered speed. "Next time," he said sagely, "don't leave it so late." He turned to go into the next car.

"I won't," she managed. "Thanks for your help."

"Och, 'twas nothing. Do ye' know your seat reservation?"

"A friend's waiting for me," she replied evasively.

"Then ye'd better let him know. He'll be thinkin' ye've missed it."

"I will," she promised. Suddenly a thought struck her. "How did you know it was a he?"

"I shouldna think ye'd run so hard unless it was," he said before he politely held the door and motioned her through. His bulky form moved purposefully through the car.

She clutched a handrail along the windows as the train moved swiftly out of the Waterloo yards. The narrow-gauge wheels chattered over the banks of switching tracks near the station.

Her teeth would sound exactly the same if she'd let them, Carolyn decided. She stood still, summoning her courage to search through the coaches and confront Mike. It was one thing to pursue a man when you were miles apart— infinitely different when you could meet him nose-to-nose any minute.

She noticed that she was collecting curious stares from the occupants of the section beside her, so she moved slowly down the car, surveying each compartment as she passed. When she reached the end of the car without encountering a familiar masculine figure, she didn't know whether to be relieved or concerned. What if she was on the wrong train? Then she shook her head to dispel such a fancy. Liz was never wrong on timetables. Mike just *had* to be on this train.

Finally—at the end of the fourth car—he was.

Caro stood limp in the corridor, scarcely able to believe her eyes.

Mike's long frame was folded into the narrow

velour seat next to the windows. Evidently he was the sole occupant of the compartment because he had carelessly thrown his topcoat and briefcase on the seats facing him. There was a London newspaper in his lap but his strong hands rested apathetically on its unopened pages. Despite an attractive view of suburban countryside through the train window, his gaze was fixed unseeingly on the empty seat in front of him.

She would remember his expression always. It was quiet, resigned, and utterly desolate.

Her tremulous smile reflected an inner glow as she reached in her bag and pulled out the Sweetheart Spoon. Mike's preoccupation was so great that he didn't even look up when she opened the compartment door and stepped inside.

It was hard to speak around the lump in her throat but she managed. "Good morning," she said. "Would you happen to have a window I could hang this in?" She held the spoon in front of her like a crusader's lance.

It's a wonder the wooden spoon ever survived the next few minutes. There was an instant of suspended animation—then Mike exploded upwards and engulfed her in an embrace that momentarily threatened both her rib cage and the spoon. She felt an instant of concern before his lips came down on hers but after that, everything blurred in a haze of complete delight.

It was enough to press closer, to savor, and to

hope that he would never take his mouth from hers. When he eventually did, she found that she was clinging to his shoulders and breathing as hard as when she had sprinted for the train.

"I'm sure I'll get used to it," she murmured ecstatically, "but you have the most shattering effect on my nervous system."

She felt his silent laughter. He said, "After we've been married long enough to get acquainted, I'll explain what effect you've had on mine."

At that moment, their British Railways engineer decided to take a curve at full speed and they were pitched onto the dusty velour seat behind them.

"I couldn't have timed it better myself," Mike told her, tightening his grip around her waist. "Let me know when we get to Southampton." He bent his head purposefully again.

"Just a minute." She pushed back an inch or so and happily noted that his clasp didn't slacken. "Mike, do you have any money?"

He peered down at her with amusement. "Well, I have a damned good job and some money sewn in the mattress at home. Why? Do I need to file a financial report with your family?"

"Idiot! I mean money for now. I'm on this train without a ticket and I don't think the conductor will cash a traveler's check."

"I promise not to let them throw you off unless they slow down for a crossing," he replied solemnly. Then his eyes darkened and he said in a tight voice, "I'd given you up. All the time we were sitting in the station, I kept staring down the platform." He made an embarrassed grimace. "It didn't seem possible that you wouldn't come eventually. Then, when the train started, it finally occurred to me that I'd been an almighty fool."

She rested her head against the warmth of his shoulder. "What were you going to do about it?"

He dropped a kiss on her forehead. "I was deciding I'd drive back to Lyonsgate from Southampton today. I had to find out if you'd agreed to marry Hugh. It was impossible to go away without knowing for sure." His grip tightened. "But this time, I was damned well going to let you hear how I felt."

"I should hope so." She brought her head up indignantly. "How in the dickens was I supposed to act when I thought you were engaged to some bosomy redhead all the time?"

"My God, you mean you didn't know!"

"Not until yesterday after you'd gone." Her voice softened as she traced her finger around the edge of his mouth. "Liz thought you'd told me. It serves you right—inventing fiancées like that. Although if you're tempted to pick up any other women on the road, you can tell them that you're engaged to a dishwater blonde with a vile temper."

"By then," he corrected, "I'll tell them that I'm married to the gorgeous blonde seated beside me with the youngest of our six children on her lap."

"Six?"

"Seven if you insist," he said magnanimously. "I was merely considering the population explosion."

She giggled. "You'd better file a financial statement after all."

"Mercenary female," he accused. The severity was tempered by his kissing her ear at the time.

"Uh-huh." Her head was nestled against his shoulder again. "Mike, what kind of furniture do you have in your house?"

"Apartment," he corrected absently. "Sort of modern, I guess. Why?"

"Because I asked Hugh to save Poppa Bear for us. I hope he'll fit in with the decor."

Mike wondered exactly what kind of surroundings *would* fit that moth-eaten rug but only for a moment. "He'll come in handy on the long winter nights," he said easily.

"In front of a roaring fire in our fireplace." She shivered as his lips marked a soft trail along her cheekbones and felt his arms tighten in response. "Oh Mike, I do love you."

"Just as it should be." His casual words didn't match the sudden roughness of his voice. He was turning her head back up to him. "Remember though, my darling Carolyn, that damned bearskin stays on the floor at home. We won't need his help anymore."

"Just as it should be. . . ." she repeated to tease him. Then his mouth descended on hers and stopped further conversation.

When the conductor came by to collect the tickets, he took one look at them and felt his ears go red. It would be better, he decided, to leave that compartment until later.

Over their heads, a poster from British Rail proclaimed "Visit Friendly Britain." The conductor winked at it solemnly, sighed with envy, and moved discreetly down the aisle.

More Romances from the SIGNET Collection

☐ **LOVE ON A HOLIDAY (originally entitled Alison Comes Home) by I. Torr.** Could Ken Macgregor protect Alison from the unknown terror that was about to engulf her? (#P5620—60¢)

☐ **ROYAL SCOT by Vivian Donald.** It began as a battle to restore the Scottish monarchy and ended in love and a flight to the heather. (#P5181—60¢)

☐ **SECRETS CAN BE FATAL by Monica Heath.** A lovely young girl accompanies a writer to a deserted mansion to work with him on his next book, not realizing that the bizarre tale he is weaving is really the story of her own past, a past she has never known. (#P5180—60¢)

☐ **MEXICAN INTERLUDE by Pamela Nichols.** (Condensed) A trio from a New York fashion magazine on assignment in Mexico becomes involved with a mysterious stranger who spells love, larceny, diamonds—and attempted murder. (#P5112—60¢)

☐ **SUNDOWN by I. Torr.** For Robina Ralston her first visit to Africa is a time of danger and excitement as she and handsome Paul Hope, the young American bookseller, are caught up in the events that threaten to overwhelm the newly independent country of Gamboney. (#P5074—60¢)

☐ **SARI by Bette Allan.** (Condensed) A young woman determined to make her mark in the world and carry on her father's business is thwarted by her sister, who maneuvers her part of the business the way she maneuvers her men—with lethal know-how. (#P5073—60¢)

EVOKE

THE

WISDOM

OF

THE

TAROT

With your own set of 78, full-color cards—the Rider-Waite deck you have studied in THE TAROT REVEALED.
